'You read my min[...] [...]
lously. 'You're try[...] [...]
because I think ab[...] [...]

J'hon's silky gloves moved, touching now the corner of Mandy's eyes, sliding down her cheek, tracing the pattern of imaginary tears.

'Yes,' she said, softly. 'It makes me sad. Thinking about Rose makes me sad. But how . . . and even if you know that, it still doesn't explain how you knew she'd been hurt.'

She shivered as the boy's hands left her face and fell to his side.

'Who are you?'

Other Corgi books for you to enjoy

PIG-HEART BOY
A.N.T.I.D.O.T.E.
HACKER
THIEF!
by Malorie Blackman

THE VANISHING HITCH-HIKER
by Roy Apps

The NOWHERE BOY

SANDRA GLOVER

CORGI BOOKS

THE NOWHERE BOY
A CORGI BOOK : 0 552 54647 X

First published in Great Britain by
Andersen Press Limited in 1997

PRINTING HISTORY
Corgi edition published 1999

Set in 12/16pt Palatino by Kestrel Data, Exeter, Devon.

Corgi Books are published by Transworld Publishers Ltd,
61–63 Uxbridge Road, London W5 5SA,
in Australia by Transworld Publishers,
c/o Random House Australia Pty Ltd,
20 Alfred Street, Milsons Point, NSW 2061,
and in New Zealand by Transworld Publishers,
c/o Random House New Zealand,
18 Poland Road, Glenfield, Auckland.

Made and printed in Great Britain by
Cox & Wyman Ltd, Reading, Berkshire.

THE NOWHERE BOY

CHAPTER ONE

They came at night. Another emergency. Mandy lay on her bed, the sound of their voices making the learning of French verbs impossible. She closed her book and listened. She knew who they were. Sue Jenson and Mike Patty. Social workers. And, though she couldn't hear their words, the message was clear enough. They had brought a child. Another girl or boy for her parents to foster. One of the temporary sisters and brothers who had been her companions for as long as she could remember.

Mandy sat up, resting her head against the pillows and considered the possibilities. What would it be, this time? A baby? She liked babies. She could make silly cooing noises at them when she felt like it but otherwise they didn't interfere with her life. Except when they kept her awake with their crying. Automatically her hand stretched out and opened the bedside drawer to check her supply of earplugs. The crying wasn't too bad. At least you could block it out and it usually meant the baby was OK.

It was the quiet ones you had to worry about. Like Billy. Billy had never cried. Not once in all the three months he had been with them. The bruises, which had covered his little body when he arrived, had healed but there was other, more serious damage. Billy had eventually moved on to permanent, adoptive parents who would care for his special needs but his vacant blue eyes haunted her still and brought tears to her own.

Tears. It nearly always ended in tears for one reason or another. The young kids were the worst. The ones who messed up your clothes and broke all your things. Last year it had been Kylie. An angelic-looking four-year-old who had used the contents of Mandy's make-up bag to paint herself, her dolls and the bedroom wall. Mum had laughed! And, in the end, Mandy had laughed too. She was torn between sadness and relief when Kylie's dad came out of hospital and was able to take her home.

Kylie had been a short-stay child. Like fifteen-year-old Ben who had locked himself in the bathroom with a canister of glue and nearly died. After that, Mum had said she wasn't having another teenager. She did, of course. Sarah, who was OK and Lucy who had 'borrowed' their car. Not that Lucy, at thirteen, knew how to drive. She had got as far as the end of the road before crashing through Mrs Henderson's privet hedge. Though hardly funny at the time, the memory made Mandy smile. Poor Mrs Henderson. She still wasn't speaking to them. She had been very fond of her privets.

Sometimes, they only had one child. At other times, three or four. Some stayed for months and, in a few cases, years. Rose was with them two years, ten months and four days. She had arrived just after her third birthday, thin, grubby and barely able to talk. On the first night, Rose had wandered into Mandy's bedroom and crawled into

9

bed with her. After that, they had squeezed a spare bed into the corner and there Rose had stayed. Mandy's devoted shadow.

It was Mandy who had taken her to speech therapy every Thursday evening after school. Mandy who had taught her to swim and ride a bike. Mandy who took her to the park and sat through Disney cartoons at the cinema with her. Mandy hadn't even minded being woken each morning by Rose's excited chatter. Each day, her words became more distinct. She was a quick learner was Rose and once she had discovered talking, she didn't stop.

Mandy looked over to the corner. The bed was empty now, save for a discarded pile of clothes. Three months ago, the courts had finally made a decision on Rose's future. She was to live with her grandmother. Not far away. Only the other side of the city somewhere. But it might as well have been Mars. Grandma would allow no contact. She wanted Rose to have a fresh start. To forget.

'Forget,' Mandy muttered out loud. 'Forget! Almost three years and we're supposed to pretend it never happened.'

She took out the photograph of Rose which she kept in her bedside cabinet. Slightly freckled cheeks. Blond hair tied up in the French plait Mandy used to do for her. Pale green eyes which never quite lost their sadness, even when Rose smiled.

Mandy slammed the photograph down. It was so unfair. So impossible. She couldn't keep going through . . . Mandy stopped mid-thought, the voices of the social workers still mingling with those of her parents. Something was wrong. They shouldn't be here. Not any more.

After Rose, she had talked to her parents and asked them to stop fostering. Amazingly, they had agreed, almost without argument. Not so much because she was upset but because she was fourteen now and starting her GCSE exam courses. She would, her dad pointed out, need a bit of peace. Her mum, too, had agreed it was a good time for a break. Within days of making the decision, she had got herself a part-time job in the supermarket and later started an Open University degree.

So what were the social workers doing here at ten o'clock on a Friday night? Mandy glanced at her French verbs and at the unfinished history essay. There was no way she was going to concentrate until she found out what was going on.

She swung her legs over the side of her bed and eased her feet into the soft, furry slippers which made no noise as she walked. She crept out of the room and hovered at the top of the stairs. The voices were clearer now.

'So how's life at the supermarket?' Sue was asking. 'How many days did you say you worked?'

An ordinary enough question but Mandy wasn't fooled. This was no social call. Mike and Sue were far too busy to call on people for a chat. This was business all right. And probably not ordinary business either. If they were hoping to get her mother out of her short retirement, then you could bet it was one of their 'special cases'. One that other foster parents didn't want, or weren't capable of taking on. A battered baby, a withdrawn waif, a neurotic drug abuser. They had had them all in their time. Mum could never resist them. And, in spite of their agreement, Mandy couldn't trust her to resist now.

She walked slowly downstairs, as her mother answered Sue's question with ominous undertones.

'Well, I only work mornings, so I suppose . . . but then, I've got OU essays to do and I have to attend tutorials once a . . . and there's not only me to consider. I mean, it was Mandy who . . .'

Oh, don't mind me, Mandy thought bitterly, staring at herself in the hall mirror, pushing strands of light brown hair behind her ears. I'll cope like I always do. Put up with its temper tantrums while it's here, cry for weeks when it goes. She stopped fiddling with her hair, as a thought struck her. What if it wasn't a new child? Sometimes, the old ones came back. What if . . . Rose . . . What if it was Rose?

She advanced silently towards the lounge, all ill humour banished in this sudden hope. She was in luck. The lounge door was open slightly. Just enough to peep in to assess the scene before committing herself to action.

As she approached, a black-and-white border collie shuffled out to greet her. Meg might be old, but her senses were still sharper than any human. Mandy put her hand down to stop the dog making too much fuss and positioned herself in the doorway.

A single glance was enough to banish all optimism. It wasn't Rose who stood, immobile in the centre of the room, her back to the door. It was an older girl, about her own age, she guessed. Dressed in black. None too clean. Dark hair tied back in a pony tail.

'I know it's awkward,' said Mike, stroking his ginger beard and leaning forward in the armchair to stare at her parents who were sitting together on the settee. 'And I take on board what you're saying, Mrs Jones.'

'Only we don't have many options,' said Sue, also leaning forward from her chair in a two-pronged attack. 'We wouldn't ask if . . .'

'No, I'm sorry,' said Mandy's mother,

rather less firmly than Mandy would have liked. 'We can't take him.'

Him! Mandy looked again. Not a girl. Oh, well, an easy mistake to make, with the pony tail and shapeless one-piece outfit it was wearing. He, not it, she corrected herself.

'Alan?' Sue said, appealing to Mandy's father.

'It's up to Cath,' came his predictable reply. 'And Mandy. We'd have to ask Mandy.'

It was time to make an entrance.

'No,' said Mandy, stepping into the room, with the dog at her heels.

The boy didn't move. Mandy had expected him to turn round. To show some interest in this new arrival. But he didn't. He continued to face Sue, forcing Mandy to cross the room and position herself by Sue's chair to get a better view. She was vaguely aware that Sue was speaking to her but Mandy's attention was already firmly fixed on the boy.

It was difficult to know which was the more striking, his face or his bizarre clothes.

He was what Mandy's friends might have called an individual dresser. The tight, black one-piece, with no obvious signs of buttons or zips, might have looked fashionable in the sixties. It was held, in the middle, by a black belt with a large silver – what? Mandy supposed it was some sort of buckle but it was solid, like a box. Round his right wrist was a thick bangle of similar solid design and on his left, one of those heavy multi-purpose digital watches which doubled as calculators. Every centimetre of his body was covered, from his feet, encased in thick, black boots, to the tips of his fingers covered by silky, black gloves. The weirdest thing, though, was that everything seemed to have a fine coating of thin, grey dust, as if the boy and his clothes had recently been taken down from a shelf where they had lain, neglected, for years.

'So we thought, if he could spend time with someone about his own age he might . . .'

'What?' said Mandy.

'His own age,' Sue repeated. 'We think he's about fourteen or fifteen.'

'Oh, yes,' Mandy muttered, before returning her attention to the boy's face.

There was something about it which disturbed her. Something she hadn't quite been able to place. It was an attractive sort of face, if you ignored the grime. High cheekbones, darkish complexion, nice straight nose, brown eyes. Brown eyes, Mandy's brain repeated. Not dark brown like Sue's nor hazel like her own. In fact, if she had to compare them to anybody's in the room, it would have to be Meg's. The boy's eyes were like the dog's. Brown, almost orange and hardly any white showing. There was far too much colour. Mandy wondered whether his vision was impaired by this strange defect. She thought not. At least not close up. He seemed to be seeing her clearly enough. His face was impassive but behind the eyes there was action. He was seeing and assessing, just as she was.

'I'm Mandy,' she said abruptly, deciding to break the silence between them which threatened to become permanent.

His head moved to one side, rather

like Meg's would have done, but he didn't reply.

'He doesn't understand English,' Sue said.

'Oh,' said Mandy.

She looked again at the dark skin. He could be anything. Italian. East European. Asian possibly.

'What does he understand?'

'Er – nothing,' said Mike. 'As far as we can make out. We've tried all the obvious ones.'

'Well, where does he come from?' Mandy asked. 'His family must speak something.'

'There isn't a family,' Sue explained. 'At least none we know about. Police picked him up, trying to break into a car in the city centre, apparently. Couldn't get a word out of him. Nothing worth charging him with, so they handed him over to us.'

'Oh,' said Mandy, again.

'He was pretty filthy when they found him.'

'Still is!' said Mandy.

'We've cleaned him up a bit,' said Mike apologetically. 'Can't get him to wash, though, or take his clothes off. Not even the gloves. We got a doctor in to examine him but the boy went wild. We'd have to sedate him to get near him and we don't really want to do that unless absolutely necessary.'

'Of course not!' said Mandy's mother. 'I'm sure he'll be fine if . . .'

She paused. Mandy raised her eyebrows in warning. This was a special case, all right. And if she didn't make her feelings very clear she'd be lumbered with a new foster brother who didn't talk and smelt like the contents of their dustbin.

'No,' she said. 'No, Mum. You promised!'

CHAPTER TWO

Mandy flopped onto the settee, next to her parents.

'How's Rose?' she asked, partly out of genuine interest and partly to prove that discussion about the boy was over.

'Well – er,' said Mike.

'Fine,' said Sue, peering at Mandy through tortoiseshell glasses, which, combined with her round face, made her look a bit like an owl.

'Under the circumstances,' said Mike. 'It's not ideal, as you know. We're keeping an eye on things.'

'Not ideal!' said Mandy. 'No. It's not. Not from what I've heard. I wouldn't leave my dog with that woman.'

'That woman,' said Mike, placidly, 'is Rose's grandmother. OK, her house may not be as clean as yours. She might not wash Rose's clothes so often, or bother to read her stories, but she's family. She has rights.'

'So does Rose,' Mandy muttered.

'Er – about the boy?' said Sue, hopefully.

'You make me sick,' Mandy snapped, ignoring the increasingly horrified glances from her parents. 'We weren't good enough for Rose, were we? And now you turn up here expecting us to . . .'

'Wait a minute,' said Mike. 'That's not fair. We supported your application to adopt Rose. You know we did. Personally, I'd have been happier if she'd stayed here. But in the end, it wasn't our decision to make. The Children Act tries to balance the rights of the natural family with the best interest of the child and in Rose's case . . .'

'Huh!' Mandy sneered. 'So it was in Rose's interests to take her away, was it? Oh, yes! I could tell by the way she screamed when she left.'

'Mandy,' said her father, gently squeezing her hand. 'It's no good going over it all again. I'm sorry,' he said to the social workers. 'You can see how it is. We can't help you. Not this time.'

The boy suddenly leant forward. It was the first time Mandy had seen him move and she instinctively pressed back against the settee, as a silky glove reached out and touched her face, brushing away the tears which had come, almost without her realizing.

'It's not us we want you to help,' said Sue, seeing this unexpected advantage. 'That's the first time we've seen him react to anything. If he could just spend a few days here . . . It's not just your parents, Mandy. It's you. You've got a real talent with these kids. The ones that don't communicate. They always open up with . . .'

Sue's voice droned on, laying it on thick, as the boy withdrew to the centre of the room. Meg wandered over and sat at his feet. Together they looked at Mandy, reproachfully. Pleading, though neither of them knew what was going on. Did they?

Mandy became aware that it was not two pairs of eyes but six, which now rested upon her. The dog started to whine.

'Oh, shut up, Meg,' she snapped. 'What do you know about it?'

'Just for a few days?' Mandy's mother asked quietly, as if to herself.

Mandy looked at the boy. A single tear had formed in the corner of his left eye and now trickled onto his cheek.

'Oh, do what you want,' said Mandy, leaping up and rushing from the room. 'Why should I care?'

That, she was still telling herself on Saturday morning, was the problem. She did care. Like them or loathe them, she could never ignore the children who passed through her life. She had never learnt to be detached, as her dad had done, nor resilient like her mum. She had lain on her bed, last night, listening to the social workers leave. Them but not the boy. Her feigned indifference had been enough. Her mum had weakened. The boy would stay.

He was already in the kitchen when she went down, still dressed in the outfit of the previous night. Mandy wondered if he had slept in it. Probably, judging by the creases. He sat at the kitchen table with a bowl of cereal in front of him.

'He won't eat,' said Mandy's mother.

A common enough problem, though mainly with the little ones.

'I've tried offering him some toast.'

'He'll eat when he's hungry,' said Mandy, sitting down opposite him and helping herself to cereal.

As she picked up her spoon, the boy did the same.

'He's just being polite,' said Mandy. 'Waiting for me, look . . . Uggh!'

As the first of her cereal slid down her throat, the boy's spilt from his mouth and dribbled onto the table.

'Mum,' she wailed. 'He's like a baby.'

'Sssh,' said her mother, grabbing her arm and dragging her away from the table. 'I expected something like this.'

'Why are you whispering? He doesn't understand.'

'He might do. We can't be sure. He doesn't speak, though. That's for sure. Sue explained after you walked out last night.'

'Explained what?'

'While he was fighting that doctor off, who tried to examine him, they caught a

24

glimpse of his mouth. His tongue's . . . er . . .'

'What?'

'Not fully developed or mutilated in some way. They think it might have been cut.'

'Cut!' Mandy screamed.

'Sssssh!'

Mandy turned back to the table. The boy was shoving cereal greedily into his mouth, enjoying the bits that stayed there. Somehow, with that and the news she'd just heard, Mandy didn't fancy her breakfast any more.

'Where's Dad?'

'Had to go into work, which is a bit of a problem. I'm working myself till lunch time so . . .'

'Terrific,' said Mandy. 'You want me to look after our friend here?'

'It's only for a couple of hours.'

'I'm supposed to be meeting Taira and Jill down the precinct. Jill needs new blades and I was going to get a . . . oh, it doesn't matter.'

Mandy stared at her mother. She wished she had a mother like some of her friends had. An irritating, unreasonable mother that you could argue with and storm out on. But her mum wasn't like that. She was so patient. So understanding. So committed to all the kids they took on. So pleasant that it sort of rubbed off on people. You found yourself doing things for Mum that you probably wouldn't do for anyone else.

'OK,' she said. 'But I'm definitely going skating at two, so don't be late back.'

'Thanks, love. If there's any problem you can phone me, or Dad, or Mike's home number.'

'I'll be fine,' said Mandy. 'Go on or you'll be late.'

She shrugged as her mother left for work. It was just as well she had to stay in. There was still the homework from last night to finish.

'I'm just popping upstairs,' she told the boy. 'Stay there.'

When she returned, most of the cereal had disappeared from the bowl. She wiped the table, sat down and opened her history books. The essay was more or less planned out. It shouldn't take long to write. She carefully drew a margin, wrote the title at the top of the page and began.

'Oh, this is hopeless,' she said, feeling the boy's eyes upon her.

He was leaning across the table, watching every move she made.

'Haven't you got anything to do? No, of course you haven't. Well, we can hardly sit and chat, can we?' she said, abandoning the essay. 'I don't even know your name. Mandy. I'm MANDY.'

She spelt it out, letter by letter. The boy's head tilted to the left.

'MANDY,' she repeated.

His head tilted to the right.

She tore a rough sheet of paper from her notebook and wrote her name.

'See,' she said, moving her seat next to the boy. 'Mandy.'

She pointed at herself.

'Mandy.'

He seemed interested, so she pointed to the dog who was curled up asleep in her basket.

'Meg. M-E-G. Meg.'

She wrote it down. The boy pointed at the dog but said nothing.

'Right. You're getting the idea, aren't you? Do you know letters? The alphabet? Look.'

She began to write down the alphabet, sounding each letter carefully. Teaching the boy as she had once taught Rose. She circled the letters of her name. Luckily it followed basic phonetic rules.

'Mandy. Yes?'

She nodded at him and the boy nodded back.

This was weird. Where had he been for fifteen years? There were kids in her class who weren't too good at reading. Some who struggled with English as their second language. But they all had some idea. This boy seemed to have none. Carefully, she went through it all again. Her name. Meg's name. The alphabet.

Suddenly, the boy grabbed the pen and notepad and began to scribble but no mark appeared. She took the pen from him.

'You hold it that way up, see?' she said, pointing the ballpoint at the paper.

She gave back the pen and waited with no hope of success. A boy who reached the age of fifteen or so without knowing which way up to hold a pen was hardly likely to be able to write. She stared, astonished, as the pad was pushed back towards her. Was this just a random series of lucky scribbles or did it mean something? There were letters written, fairly distinctly in the top corner.

J'hon.

'John,' she said, beaming at him. 'Your name is John?'

She nodded at him.

He nodded and smiled. Then he grabbed the pen and paper back and began to write. Within minutes the paper was covered. The words Mandy, Meg and J'hon filled every line.

'Good,' she said. 'Very good. Shall I show you how to spell John properly?'

She tore off another sheet and wrote it down.

'J'hon,' the boy wrote back.

'Oh, well, I suppose the individual spelling goes with the individual dress sense.

Did you go to one of these progressive schools or what? Come on, let's try some more words.'

By the time her mother returned, Mandy felt she had made considerable progress. J'hon was able to write and seemed to understand about fifty simple words.

'It's weird,' Mandy told her mum. 'He seems bright enough. You'd swear he was really intelligent but he knows nothing. Not even how to hold a pen properly. Do you reckon he could have amnesia or something?'

'Lost memory would explain a lot,' said her mother. 'Maybe when he settles we can get him checked out at the doctor's. Perhaps he's had a bump on the head. An accident of some sort. But the main thing for now is to get his trust. You seem to be doing a good job.'

Mandy had, in fact, started to enjoy herself and nothing but the thought of ice-skating could have torn her away.

'Your turn now,' she said. 'I'm going to get ready.'

It didn't take long. Mandy liked to look

good but could rarely be bothered with make-up and her straight hair was cut to chin length, so it wasn't too much trouble.

She appeared in the kitchen with her jacket on, ready to go. Her mother was making sandwiches and J'hon was flicking through Mandy's homework books.

'You won't understand much of that,' she told him. 'I barely do myself. Don't make lunch for me, Mum. I'll grab a burger at the rink.'

J'hon looked at her, briefly, before his eyes turned to the wall, or more specifically to the phone which hung there. He stared, nervously, as if he expected it to leap off the wall and attack him. When it didn't, he edged towards it, stretched out his hand and touched it.

'Phone,' said Mandy. 'It's a telephone.'

J'hon lifted the receiver, put it to his ear, shook it and put it down again.

'Seems to know what to do with . . .'

Mandy never finished. The phone rang. J'hon who was still hovering by it, let out a terrified shriek and rushed from the room.

'Oh heck,' said Mandy. 'You answer it. I'll go and see what he's up to.'

She followed him upstairs. The shriek had proved one thing, at least. He could make sounds, even if he couldn't form them into words.

She found him in his bedroom, curled on his bed, his gloved fist in his mouth.

'It's OK,' she said, sitting down beside him. 'It's only the telephone. You must have come across phones before, surely? What is it? Do you think the call's about you? Have you run away from somewhere . . . or what?'

The questions were addressed to herself. She hadn't expected an answer and the boy's only reply was to grasp her hand firmly in his own.

CHAPTER THREE

Rose knocked and pushed open the door of her grandmother's room.

'Gran,' she whispered.

No reply.

'Babs,' she said, hesitantly, remembering that she didn't like to be called Gran.

She had put up with it for the first few days before snapping, 'For God's sake, Rose. You make me feel ancient. Call me Babs, like everyone else does.'

It was hard to get used to. Mandy's grandma didn't mind being called Gran. Not even by Rose. But then Babs wasn't like Mandy's gran. Babs's hair was blond, not grey. She wore bright red lipstick. Even now, while she slept.

'Babs,' Rose repeated, touching her shoulder, gently.

No movement.

Rose picked up a bottle that lay on the

crumpled covers. The white pills rattled but still Babs didn't stir. Rose put the bottle on top of a pile of tissues, magazines and empty cigarette packets which cluttered the bedside table.

'I'm hungry,' she said.

One dull, blue eye opened.

'Get something to eat then,' Babs groaned, rolling over on to her back and snoring loudly.

Rose wandered downstairs. It was cold. Mandy's house was never cold. It was nice there. But she couldn't go back. Mandy didn't want her any more. Rose stood in the narrow hall and tugged at a piece of damp wallpaper which was hanging off the wall. What had she done? How had she upset Mandy? Was it because she had dropped that plate? She was only helping to wash up. And Mandy hadn't seemed cross at the time. Was it because she had lost those mittens Mandy's mum had knitted? Couldn't be. The mittens had turned up in the lost property box at school. Her old school that was. She went to a different school now. When Babs remembered to take her. That lady – Sue – had been cross last week when she had come round.

'She's got to go to school,' she'd said. 'If you can't manage I'll . . .'

'I can manage,' Babs had screamed. 'Brought up four of my own, didn't I? Kid felt sick, this mornin'. That's why I didn't send her. Felt sick, didn't yer, Rose?'

It was true. Sort of. She felt sick most of the time now. But she liked to go to school. Was she supposed to be there today? Maybe not. It was Saturday, wasn't it?

'What the hell are you doing?'

Rose looked at the man, framed in the kitchen doorway. Babs's friend. The one she was supposed to call Uncle Joe. The one who smelt of beer and had dirt under his fingernails.

'Leave the bloody wallpaper alone, will yer?'

Rose dropped the piece of paper and scurried past him into the kitchen. He didn't follow. She heard him stamping upstairs. On the kitchen table lay a plate, a mug, an open newspaper and a box of matches. Rose picked up a crust of toast

35

from the plate and nibbled it. She sat down, pulling the newspaper towards her. It was not one she had seen before. It was different from the ones at Mandy's house. Smaller but with bigger letters and more pictures. Mandy. Mandy. Why hadn't Mandy been to see her? What had that lady said? The one called Sue. Something about her and Mandy not being real sisters.

'But I could be,' Rose shouted aloud. 'I could try. I could try to be a real sister. I'll try, Mandy. Please, Mandy. Let me come home. I'll try.'

Mandy felt the grip on her hand tighten.

'What is it?' she said, as the boy's strange eyes stared wildly round the room.

He leapt up, dragging her with him, stopping outside her own room.

'In there,' she said. 'You want to go in there?'

He had already kicked open the door and stood, looking into the room, as if expecting to see someone. A flicker of confused disappointment crossed his serious features. He released her hand.

'Boy, are you weird,' said Mandy, shivering. 'Come on.'

She went downstairs, meeting her mother at the bottom.

'Is he OK?'

'Sort of,' said Mandy. 'But you're not. What's wrong?'

'Now, don't panic, Mandy,' said her mother, causing Mandy's stomach to do a quick somersault. 'That was the hospital on the phone. Your gran's had a fall. But she's all right. Her hip's broken.'

'Broken!' said Mandy. 'That's not my idea of all right. Oh, heck . . . I suppose we'll have to take J'hon with us.'

'Where?'

'To the hospital.'

'No, it's best if I go on my own, I think. You know Gran. She'll only moan at me for dragging you away from your precious skating.'

'Yes, but . . . I can't go skating with poor Gran . . . and what about him? We can't leave him here.'

'Couldn't you take him with you?'

Mandy looked at J'hon's grubby clothes.

It wouldn't do much for her image turning up at the rink with someone like that.

'It'd be a big help.'

'Suppose so,' said Mandy, reluctantly. 'If you really don't think I should come to the hospital.'

'No, you can go tomorrow, if Gran's feeling up to it. Don't worry, I'll give her your love.'

'Come on, then,' Mandy said to J'hon. 'I don't know what Jill and Taira are going to make of you.'

J'hon, in fact, did not look so out of place in the queue of people lined up outside the ice-rink. A lot of the skaters wore dark clothes and almost all of them wore gloves. Even the silver box at his waist looked like a fancy version of the money belts many of Mandy's friends carried.

'This is John,' she said, skipping the queue to join Jill and Taira, who were at the front. 'Don't worry if he acts a bit strange. We think he's lost his memory or something.'

She didn't mention the other oddities. She was too exhausted for a start, after all the trouble she'd had getting him to the rink. He'd gone crazy when she'd tried to get him on a bus and she'd had to let three go by before she finally managed it.

'He won't understand you,' she told Taira, who was asking whether he could skate. 'Doesn't talk, either.'

'Who needs conversation,' Jill whispered, 'when you look like that? He's gorgeous – in a Heathcliff sort of way!'

They were reading *Wuthering Heights* at school and, on reflection, Mandy had to admit that J'hon was a bit like Emily Brontë's anti-hero. Appearing out of nowhere. Dark, brooding and decidedly uncommunicative!

The queue started to move, preventing further discussion of J'hon's qualities. The girls had their own skates but Mandy got a skate hire ticket for J'hon. She sat down with him on one of the low benches and pointed to his feet.

'You have to take your boots off,' she told him. 'And change them for skates.'

She pointed to her own skates, bent down and tried to pull his boots. He leapt up and cowered against the wall as if she'd hit him. Patiently, she took off her own shoes.

'See?' she said. 'Off. Shoes off feet.'

J'hon didn't move.

'You go,' she told her friends. 'I'll sort him out.'

She waited until the changing room was almost empty, before having a word with the lad who worked at the skate hire counter. He knew Mandy and handed over a pair of skates, without taking any shoes in return.

'Look,' she said to J'hon. 'You have to put these on feet.'

Five minutes later, she abandoned the struggle.

'OK,' she said. 'You can just watch. Come on.'

She positioned J'hon at the side of the rink and slid, effortlessly, onto the ice. She was an excellent skater. Every Sunday she had lessons but the Saturday afternoon sessions were just for fun. She caught up with her friends and skated round, chatting. Every few minutes she glanced at the side, to see if J'hon was still there.

'Oh, heck, where's he gone?' she said after half a dozen circuits of the rink.

She found him in the changing rooms, wrestling with the long laces on the skates she'd given him.

'Good,' she said. 'You're going to have a go. Here, I'll do it.'

He let her lace up the skates, without fuss and even allowed her to hand in his boots to the attendant. She grabbed his arm and helped him totter to the edge of the rink. She summoned her friends. Eager to help, they grabbed an arm each leaving Mandy redundant, as they steered J'hon onto the ice.

She watched them make the first, hesitant, tour of the rink, laughing, as J'hon slithered along between them. He seemed to be doing OK, for a beginner, so Mandy stopped worrying and set off on her own.

The next time she saw him, he was managing with only one assistant.

'Let him try on his own,' she told Jill.

Jill let go of his arm. J'hon stopped for

a moment, got his balance and began to skate.

'He's good!' said Jill. 'He must have done it before. He's really confident now, look. No hassle!'

'Where's Taira?'

'In the middle, practising that jump she was struggling with last week.'

Mandy looked into the centre of the rink, where a few of the kids who had lessons were spinning and jumping with varying degrees of success.

'There she is,' said Jill. 'Just getting up. Oh, dear. What's your friend doing?'

J'hon had skated into the centre and was standing, with his head to one side, watching the proceedings.

'Oh, no!' Jill screamed. 'He's not going to try to . . . Mandy, stop him . . . he'll hurt . . .'

Mandy had already set off but she was too late. J'hon had started a spin. A beautifully controlled spin. Fast, not moving from the spot. A spin which would not have looked out of place at the British championships.

'He's definitely done this before!' said Jill, skidding to a halt beside Mandy.

'Come off it,' said Mandy. 'He didn't even know how to lace his boots up.'

'So how do you explain that?'

J'hon had taken control of the centre rink. Everyone else had stopped, forming a wide circle round him. Mandy pushed her way to the front just in time to see J'hon do a double axel. An effortless jump. A perfect landing. He followed it with a triple toe-loop.

The crowd cheered and pressed back to give him more room. A couple of the rink attendants skated up to see what was going on just as J'hon started a triple – no, not just a triple – a combination jump. Mandy had seen guys in the World Championships struggle with stuff like that.

'Stop it,' said Mandy, skating towards him. 'Stop it.'

She pulled him away, as the crowd groaned in complaint. She didn't know why, but somehow she knew he shouldn't be drawing attention to himself like this.

'Hey, who are you?' one of the attendants

said. 'What's going on? Is this some publicity stunt, or what?'

'He's Russian,' said Mandy, gibbering the first unlikely thing that popped into her mind. 'On tour . . . starts down South on Monday. Got to go . . . see yer.'

Could be true, Mandy thought, as she dragged a bewildered J'hon off the ice. He could be Russian, for all she knew. Maybe he'd got split up from his company. She resolved to check the papers to see if any Russian ice-skaters had gone missing recently. But somehow, she thought not.

'You're early,' said her dad when she got home. 'Problems?'

'You wouldn't believe it if I told you,' said Mandy. 'Mum back yet?'

'No. She's staying on at the hospital for a bit. Don't panic. Your gran's bearing up. But I'm supposed to go and pick up some things for her and deliver them to the hospital. Nightdress, reading glasses, that sort of stuff. Are you going out tonight?'

'There's a disco at school but I think I'll

give it a miss. I'm shattered. Besides, I thought I'd try and get our friend here to clean up a bit. He's starting to smell a bit too powerful.'

CHAPTER FOUR

Rose sank back in her chair, sucking a lolly and staring at the television. Uncle Joe sat on the settee, drinking a can of beer, swearing at the horses that romped across the TV screen. Next to him, Babs was painting her nails.

The horse racing ended and some ice-skating began. Rose sat up. Uncle Joe pressed the remote control and the skaters were replaced by men in striped jerseys hurling a ball around.

'Babs,' said Rose, slowly. 'Will I ever be able to go to the ice-skating again?'

'Skatin'?' muttered Babs. 'What d'yer want to go skatin' for?'

'Mandy goes skating. She taught . . .'

'Will yer shut up about bloomin' Mandy. It's all right for them,' she said, shaking her nails and lighting a cigarette. 'They've got the money for skatin' and stuff. We 'aven't.

They got paid for keepin' you, yer know.'

'Did they?'

'Yeah. But I don't. So don't keep pesterin' for things.'

'Sorry.'

'We're going out ternight, Rose,' Babs said after a while. 'Y'el be all right, won't yer?'

'I don't know.'

'Course yer will. Big girl like you. I'll put a video on for yer and leave yer some biscuits and a drink. OK? It's only fer an hour. I've got ter get out, fer God's sake. Don't look at me like that, Rose. Yer just like yer mother, you are. Always whingeing about summat.'

'I want to see my mum. When can I see her?'

Babs raised her thinly pencilled eyebrows at Joe.

'Would yer credit it?' she said. 'Girl don't listen to nothin'. Yer can't see yer mum, Rose. She's dead.'

'No she isn't,' said Rose, leaping up from the chair. 'She isn't. She isn't. Don't say that.'

'Look, Rose,' said Babs, more gently. 'I don't like it, no more than you do. She was me daughter, after all. But you have to face it, love . . .'

'Not HER,' shrieked Rose. 'I don't mean her. I mean Cath. My proper mum.'

'Can't yer shut the kid up,' Joe moaned. 'I'm trying to watch.'

'Shut it, yerself,' said Babs. 'Listen, Rose. Cath's not yer real mum. Yer proper mum was killed in a er – sort of accident. And yer dad – well, he's in prison, 'cos of yer mum's accident. It was them social workers' fault. I always wanted to look after yer but they said I weren't fit. Well, I showed 'em. I got yer back, didn't I? I look after yer proper, don't I? Never 'urt yer, 'ave I?'

Rose nodded, then shook her head. She didn't know what she was supposed to say. Babs got cross sometimes and smacked her. But not a lot. Most of the time she was nice. Gave her lots of sweets and baked beans most nights for tea. Let her go out to play a lot, too, on the street with other kids. At Mandy's she'd always had to play in the garden. Mandy's mum said the streets weren't safe. Things were different at Mandy's.

'Come here. Come and 'ave a cuddle,' said Babs, seeing tears welling up in Rose's eyes.

Babs looked at Joe for support but he was watching TV. She wondered what was wrong with Rose. She was always crying. Always feeling ill. Usually when her and Joe wanted to go out. At first, she'd given in. Stayed home with Rose. But Joe was getting fed up. And to be honest, she was too. It wasn't right to be stuck in night after night. It was nice having Rose around, but she couldn't let the kid ruin her life. Joe had said that.

'Come here,' she said again, stretching her arms out to Rose. 'I love yer. Yer know that, don't yer?'

Rose clambered onto the settee and felt Babs's arms tighten round her. Her dressing-gown felt nice and warm. She nearly always wore the dressing-gown except when she went out. She was going out later. Rose's eyes, still stinging with tears, gently closed.

Mandy threw a pile of clothes onto J'hon's bed. They always had spare clothes lying about for emergencies. Later, if the boy stayed, they would buy some new ones. But, for now, she had sorted out a pair of blue jeans and a sweater. She had also taken an Action Man doll from the toy box. She removed its clothes and headed towards the bathroom, where she had filled a bath of foamy water.

'See,' she said putting the doll into the water and washing it with a sponge. 'Wash.'

She dried the doll on a towel.

'Dry. Towel,' she said.

Then she dressed the doll and sniffed.

'Mmmmmm,' she said. 'Nice. Clean.'

She nodded at J'hon, who nodded back enthusiastically. Mandy turned to leave the bathroom before he started to undress but he grabbed her arm.

Excitedly, he snatched the doll, removed its clothes and dipped it in the water. He looked so pleased with himself, that Mandy barely knew what to do.

'No,' she said, shaking her head and pointing at the doll. 'Not it! YOU.'

J'hon looked at her in confusion and disbelief, as she pointed to him. How to explain? She could hardly demonstrate herself. She searched her mind, wondering whether they had any films on video, which featured people taking a bath.

An idea struck her and she grabbed a book from the shelf in the hall. It was a children's book entitled *First Words*. She found a picture of a little boy sailing a boat in the bath. J'hon looked at the picture and then at the bowl of bath toys they kept for younger children. He picked up a boat and put it in the water.

'Oh, heck,' said Mandy. 'This is going to take longer than I thought.'

She left the bathroom, closing the door on J'hon, hoping that he might somehow get the idea. She went downstairs, threw some mince, onions and tomatoes into a pan and got out some pasta shells. Her parents would be hungry when they returned. Not to mention herself. She hadn't eaten since breakfast. Even the tin of dog food she opened for Meg looked appetizing. She grabbed an apple to stave off the hunger pains and went to look for J'hon. She found him outside the bathroom.

'Brill,' she said, smiling in genuine admiration.

He had obviously managed to wash and had dressed himself in the jeans and sweater. He looked a bit odd with the belt, bangle and gloves on, but it was a definite improvement. No matter that the bathroom resembled a swamp and that grey murky water filled the bath. That could be dealt with. She picked up the discarded catsuit between thumb and forefinger and dropped it into the laundry basket.

'We'll wash that tomorrow,' she said. 'Come on. I can hear Mum and Dad.'

Her parents assured her that Gran was all right, congratulated J'hon on his improved appearance and sat down to their dinner. Mandy gave J'hon a spoon and waited for a fountain of Bolognese sauce to come shooting out of his mouth onto the table. It didn't. J'hon's method of eating was a little unconventional – pushing the spoon deep into his throat. But he had obviously developed a system which suited him and the meal was a relatively civilized affair.

Mandy went to her room to finish her homework, while her parents took J'hon into the lounge to watch television. She had finished the essay and just about convinced herself that she had a reasonable grasp of the French verbs, when J'hon appeared at the door.

'You can come in,' she said. 'I've finished.'

She was never certain how much he understood but talked to him anyway.

'Talk to her as much as you can,' Rose's speech therapist had said. 'They learn by listening.' J'hon wandered towards her desk and picked up the history essay.

'My homework,' she said, taking it off him and putting it in her bag. 'Hey, I've got an idea.'

She pulled out an atlas.

'Let's see if you recognize anything. Britain,' she said, pointing to a map. 'Bradford. Where we live, yes? Mandy lives in Bradford. Meg lives in Bradford. Yes?

J'hon. Where does J'hon live?'

His head tilted to the side in the manner she found both appealing and irritating.

'OK, we'll broaden our outlook a bit, shall we? The world. This is a map of the world. Russia?' she said, hopefully. 'Italy? India? Well, you must be from somewhere!'

Maybe, he just didn't understand maps. She tried again, this time lifting a small globe from the top shelf. It wasn't very detailed but at least he might be able to pinpoint the right continent.

This time, she got a reaction. J'hon snatched the globe from her hands and spun it round and round, allowing one gloved finger to slide across it as he did so.

'Traveller,' said Mandy. 'Is that what you're telling me? You don't belong anywhere? You travel, yes?'

But what sort of traveller? A gypsy? One of those New Age hippies? An entertainer? That was it! How stupid. Why hadn't she thought of it before? It all made sense. His crazy clothes. Obvious athletic ability. The circus. J'hon was from the circus. It had been in Bradford, only a week ago. One of those politically correct things with no animals and lots of acrobats. Performers from all over the world.

She grabbed a pencil and quickly sketched a circus ring on her notepad.

'Circus. Yes?' she said, pushing the pad towards him.

He took it, added a few squiggles here and there and nodded.

'Mum,' Mandy yelled, grabbing the pad and bounding downstairs. 'I've got it. Look. I've got it. J'hon's from the circus.'

She shoved the clumsy drawing under her mother's nose, while breathlessly explaining how she came to such a conclusion.

'Well done, Sherlock Holmes!' said her father.

'Looks more like a flying saucer than a circus,' said her mother. 'But you could be right. I'll give Sue a ring, so they can get onto it straight away. Should be easy enough to check.'

'Do you think we should?' said Mandy,

worried now that her original excitement had evaporated. 'Maybe he doesn't want to be found. Maybe he's run away. What if someone hurt him . . . you know . . . the tongue . . .'

'Well, whatever happened, the authorities need to find out,' said her dad. 'We have to tell them what we know and then it's up to them. It's not our decision to make, love.'

'It never is, is it?' said Mandy, bitterly. 'I'm going to bed. You'd better sort J'hon out with some pyjamas.'

It was dark when Rose woke up. The television was off, the curtains closed. A light blinked from the video machine. 23:23. What did that mean? Was that the time? Mandy had been teaching her to tell the time but she hadn't quite grasped it. Was that why Mandy didn't want her any more? Was she stupid? Joe called her stupid sometimes.

She dragged herself off the settee, switched on the light and looked around for the biscuits and pop Babs had promised.

Nothing. She went to the kitchen. Nothing there either. At least not on the table. She opened the cupboard, found some cornflakes and ate them straight from the box. She wasn't tired any more. She must have slept a long, long time. Maybe Babs was in bed. She went upstairs and checked the bedroom. Empty. The whole house was empty and very, very quiet.

She went into the bathroom and sat on the toilet. What if there were ghosts? Ghosts came at night. When it was quiet. When you were all alone. And bad men. They came at night, too. There had been a bad man, once. Someone who shouted a lot and hit her and made her cry. The stair creaked. Rose leapt up. It creaked again. Something was out there. On the stairs. She edged forward towards the door, hardly daring to breathe. It was out there. On the landing. She couldn't hear it but she knew it was there. Coming closer.

'Mandy!' she screamed. 'Mandy!'

Rose darted forward, slamming the bathroom door. But she was too late. It was in.

Brushing past her legs. Rose screamed and fell, banging her head on the side of the bath, as the startled cat let out a shriek and leapt onto the sink.

CHAPTER FIVE

It was the bedroom door bursting open that woke Mandy. She sat up and switched on the bedside lamp.

'What the . . . what time is it?' she groaned.

She glanced at her clock.

'Midnight! J'hon, what on earth do you think you're doing?'

The boy stood in the doorway, the silver buckle of his belt gleaming, incongruously fastened around a pair of her dad's pyjamas. He was clutching his head and wailing, like an injured beast.

'Have you had a nightmare?' she said, getting up and putting on her dressing-gown. 'Fallen out of bed? Ssssh . . . you'll wake the street, carrying on like that. Come on. Go back to bed.'

He shook his head, resisting her attempts to push him out of the room.

'Well, you can't stay here,' she said. 'You're not a kid . . . you're . . . well . . . you shouldn't be in my room, at night, that's all.'

Mandy knew what she meant but it sounded stupid. His intentions, whatever they were, were certainly not of an amorous nature. Nor did he seem inclined to violence. He was just lost and confused, like Rose had been that night she had clambered into Mandy's bed.

J'hon suddenly stopped wailing, nodded at her and left as quickly as he had arrived. Mandy got into bed. He sure was weird. She wondered if he was using drugs of some sort. Maybe he kept them in that silver pouch. She'd try to take a look sometime. She turned off the lamp. Minutes later the room was lit again. This time from the overhead light. J'hon was back. He was clutching a book.

Before she could move, he came and sat on the edge of the bed, dropping the book on her quilt.

'What are you doing with that?' she said, irritably.

She was tired and this was getting beyond a joke. She didn't want to be reading one of her dad's gardening books in the middle of the night.

J'hon flicked over the pages and pushed it towards her. Mandy stared at the glossy picture, trying to take it in. It was a rose.

She had been thinking of . . . had she said the name aloud? No. She was certain she hadn't. And even if . . . he wouldn't have understood . . . it was coincidence. Her head throbbed with tiredness and unanswered questions. She rubbed her forehead as she gazed at the picture.

J'hon nodded at her excitedly, rubbing his own head.

'Headache,' she said. 'You've got a headache? What the heck have headaches got to do with roses?'

The boy began to wail.

'Mum!' Mandy called. 'Mum! I think you'd better come and sort this one out.'

J'hon was still in bed when Mandy got up the following morning. Hardly surprising, as it was only seven o'clock and he had been up half the night, howling, while Mandy's mum tried to calm him down. Mandy's dad gave her a lift to her skating lesson. She told him about the night's activities, missing out a few details that her brain couldn't cope with at such an early hour.

It was almost midday when she returned. She had stayed on at the rink to watch Taira's lesson and cadge a lift home with them. It had been a bit embarrassing fending off questions from the staff about her Russian friend but, on the whole, she thought she had lied quite creditably.

'We've had quite a morning,' her mother informed her.

'Where's J'hon?' said Mandy, anxiously. 'And Dad?'

'Your dad's over at the hospital. That was the first of our crises. Gran phoned to say she wanted some more stuff taking over. Apparently she doesn't think much of the hospital soap and wanted her own. And J'hon bolted upstairs when the social workers turned up.'

'Social workers? On a Sunday? What did they want?'

'Two things, really. They checked out the circus connection.'

'And?'

'Nothing. Nobody's missing. At least they're not admitting to anyone. Police are doing a bit of an investigation. Just in case.'

'And the other thing?'

'Ah . . . they got a call from the hospital this morning. Same one your gran's in. Rose has had an accident . . .'

'Rose!' Mandy screamed. 'What?'

'It's OK, love. Calm down. She fell, apparently. Late last night. Cut her head on the side of the bath. Couple of stitches, that's all. They're keeping her in till they know exactly what happened.'

'I can imagine!'

'Mandy. We mustn't make judgements . . .'

'You don't have to,' Mandy snapped. 'I'll make up my own mind, thanks. Which ward is she in? I'm going to see her.'

'You can't,' said her mother, patiently. 'And even if you could, do you really think it would help Rose, to see you? It'd only upset her, love. You know it would.'

'He knew,' said Mandy, quietly.

'What?'

'J'hon. He knew. Last night. All that wailing and rubbing his head . . . and the book. He knew about Rose, Mum.'

'Oh, come on!' said her mother. 'That's crazy. You're upset. You're letting your imagination . . . I mean how could he?'

'I don't know,' said Mandy. 'But I'm going to find out.'

She went upstairs and knocked on J'hon's door. No answer. She pushed the door open. He wasn't there. From along the corridor, she could hear faint sounds. They were coming from her room. She crept quietly and stood in the doorway. J'hon was sitting on her bed, surrounded by a pile of debris. She saw one black, silky glove, but the rest was rather more difficult to identify. Bits of grey plastic, a couple of red buttons, batteries . . .

'Oh, no!' she said, as her empty bedside cabinet confirmed her suspicions. 'Mum!'

'What is it now?' said her mother, as Mandy bounced back into the kitchen.

'He's taken all the stuff off my cabinet – Walkman, Gameboy, alarm clock . . .'

'Well, he won't harm them.'

'He already has,' Mandy shrieked. 'He's taken them apart. It's all mixed up . . . I'll never be able to . . .'

'All right . . . it's not the end of . . .'

'Don't say it,' said Mandy. 'Spare me the lecture. Just go and look.'

Mandy hated it when they messed up her room and her mother's comment was always the same. It didn't matter. People were more important than things. Things could be replaced. Mandy knew she was right but it didn't make any difference. She still got mad.

She followed her mother upstairs and found her hovering outside the room, looking confused.

'Mandy . . . I think . . . well, you must have been mistaken.'

'Mistaken!' screamed Mandy, pushing past her into the bedroom. 'Look at it! Look what he's done!'

Her mother looked. Mandy looked. J'hon was sitting on the bed, playing with a perfectly functional Gameboy. On the cabinet, the alarm clock showed the correct time and beside it lay the Walkman, all in one piece. There wasn't a thing out of place.

'But he . . . but I . . .'

'I'll make some lunch,' said her mother, shrugging her shoulders. 'Perhaps you ought to have a lie down, love. Do you want . . . ?'

'No, I'm fine,' said Mandy. 'I think.'

She waited until she heard her mother's footsteps going downstairs and then turned on J'hon.

'OK,' she said. 'What's going on? I didn't imagine it, did I? And don't play dumb with me. You understand, don't you?'

He nodded.

'Have you always understood?'

He shook his head.

'So, let me get this right . . . you've learnt a new language in . . . er . . . about two days?'

He nodded again.

'Can you speak?'

He shook his head.

'Fine. Just carry on nodding and shaking. You took my stuff apart. Yes. And put it back together again in the time it took me to go and get Mum. Don't nod at me! It's not possible! Nobody could do that.'

The boy hung his head.

'I'm sorry,' said Mandy. 'I know you didn't mean any harm. You're just so . . . odd, that's all. I mean, last night, for a start . . . you were trying to tell me something, weren't you? About Rose?'

He nodded.

'But you couldn't . . . you don't even know Rose. You don't know anything about her.'

J'hon leapt up, shaking his head wildly, and stood opposite Mandy, close enough to touch. He put his hands on Mandy's temples and smiled.

'You read my mind,' said Mandy, incredulously. 'You're trying to say you know Rose because I think about her?'

J'hon's silky gloves moved, touching now the corner of Mandy's eyes, sliding down her cheek, tracing the pattern of imaginary tears.

'Yes,' she said, softly. 'It makes me sad. Thinking about Rose makes me sad. But how . . . and even if you know that, it still doesn't explain how you knew she'd been hurt.'

She shivered as the boy's hands left her face and fell to his side.

'Who are you?'

'Mandy! Lunch. Come on or we'll be late for the hospital.'

It was a con trick. It had to be, Mandy thought, as she nibbled her sandwiches. But why? What was the boy trying to do? He must have understood all along, of course. Must have heard her asking the social workers about Rose but that still didn't explain . . .

'Aren't you hungry, love?'

Mandy shook her head and finally abandoned the sandwich. J'hon ate his lunch, apparently unconcerned. He showed some anxiety when Mandy's dad returned and she and her mother put on their coats.

'We're going to see Gran,' Mandy explained. 'You're staying with Dad.'

Her gran was better than she had expected. Cross with herself for doing something so stupid as tripping over a box at the supermarket and debating whether to sue them for leaving it lying around.

'Just going to the loo,' Mandy said, as Gran's long story came to an end.

The toilet had been her original idea but when she failed to find it and found herself facing a sign which said 'Children's Ward' the temptation was too great. She wouldn't try to see Rose. That wasn't allowed and, like Mum said, might only upset her. But . . . She didn't really know what she was going to do as she climbed the stairs and pushed open the heavy swing doors.

'Can I help you?' asked a young nurse at the reception desk.

'Er – I just popped in to see how Rose Hutchins was doing.'

'First door on the left,' said the nurse. 'It's a bit crowded. She's doing well for visitors today.'

Mandy sidled along the corridor, keeping close to the wall. Luckily the nurse had returned to her paperwork and failed to notice Mandy's bizarre, crab-like shuffle. Mandy paused outside the room. She would allow herself just one quick peep. So quick, in fact, that she barely had time to take in what she saw. Rose was sitting up in bed and looked well enough. That was the main thing. Sue and Mike were there. Another man, staring out of the window. And a blonde woman who must be Rose's grandmother. Mandy had never seen her before and she looked too young to be anybody's grandmother but then, if she remembered correctly, Babs wasn't yet forty. Younger than Mandy's mum! It was the blonde woman who was speaking now. Had to be. It wasn't Sue's voice.

'Don't know what she was doing out of bed, daft sausage. Running about in the bathroom like that, at two in the mornin'. Good job I heard the crash, wasn't it, Rose? But you don't remember, do yer, luv? Out cold she was, when I picked her up . . .'

Mandy had heard enough. She stamped back along the corridor and out through the swing doors. Running about, indeed! Two in the morning! Who did she think she was kidding? Sue and Mike wouldn't be taken in by that story. Surely?

CHAPTER SIX

Mandy's mother didn't seem to think she'd been long at the toilet, so there was no need to mention her escapade. They sat with Gran for a while longer, until she dozed off.

All was peaceful when they got home. Dad was reading a newspaper and J'hon was watching a programme about cars on television.

'No problems with – er . . .' Mandy asked nervously, glancing at J'hon.

'No,' said her dad. 'Not really. We took Meg for a walk in the woods. I've only just got back. It was a bit strange. J'hon kept stopping to look at things. Touching trees and picking stones up. Like a toddler, really. He seems so immature in some ways but then in others . . . I can't make him out at all.'

'You don't say! Speaking of which, what's happening about tomorrow?'

'Tomorrow?'

'School.'

'Ah,' said Mandy's mother. 'I meant to tell you. They're trying to fix J'hon up with a special school but there aren't any places at the moment, so your headmistress said she'd try him in mainstream for a week or two. I think I've got something that might pass as a uniform, if we can get him into it.'

J'hon made no fuss about putting on the uniform the following morning, with a few little extras of his own. Nothing they could say would make him remove the belt, bangle and gloves. Mandy eventually got him to pull his jumper down over the belt. The gloves she would have to explain as best she could. The teachers wouldn't fuss. They were used to Mandy's foster brothers and sisters drifting in and out of school with their sometimes bizarre behaviour. The other lads would be more of a problem. They didn't like oddities. People who didn't conform were picked on. She would have to keep an eye on J'hon.

It was easy at first. As his date of birth was unknown, the headmistress put him into Mandy's class but as soon as lessons began they were split up. Mandy was in the top set for maths. J'hon, with his speech problem and no previous school records, was sent to Set 5.

Half way through the lesson, he arrived at Mandy's maths group, accompanied by the headmistress. Mandy groaned, rolling her eyes at Taira.

'Trouble already,' she whispered.

She was sitting near the front and strained to hear what the headmistress was saying to their teacher, Mrs Kingsley, who was the Head of the maths department.

'Jeff Woolcott says he can't teach him.'

'That bad, eh?' said Mrs Kingsley frowning at J'hon.

'On the contrary. He's convinced the boy's a mathematical genius. Completed assessments 1–8 faster than Jeff could check them, apparently. Trouble is, he's got no language skills. Writing's basic, speech non-existent, as you know. He'll need a special work programme.'

'All right,' said Mrs Kingsley. 'Leave him

here. I'll keep him over break and check him out.'

Mrs Kingsley's findings were the same as her colleague's. J'hon was good with numbers. Very good. In science, he was able to follow instructions, working on an experiment with Jill and Mandy, but he couldn't write up the reults. In the afternoon, the English teacher banished J'hon to the remedial specialist. At the end of the day, the headmistress sent for Mandy and asked her a lot of questions she couldn't answer.

Though determined to find out some answers, Mandy's progress was slow. With homework, cello, skating practice and visits to Gran to fit in at night, she had very little time to talk to J'hon. By the middle of the week, he had learnt to communicate by simple written messages like 'I walk Meg take' and 'Where go you'. On Friday night, he wrote a message of a different sort.

Mandy had been at Taira's working on a survey they were doing in English. She didn't get home until ten o'clock and when she did, she found the note, written in J'hon's distinctive scrawl, lying on her bed.

'What does this mean?' she said, bursting into his room. ' "Rose call". Did she phone? Did Rose phone?'

He shook his head.

'Well she couldn't have called round. Mum would have said something, so what . . .'

J'hon touched his ears and the side of his head.

'You heard her? In your head? You heard Rose?'

He nodded. Mandy was surprised to find she believed him.

'So what did she say? Is she in trouble?'

J'hon grabbed a piece of paper and wrote Mandy's name over and over.

'She's calling for me! But I don't know where – OK – I'll sort something out.'

She went downstairs. Her parents were watching the end of the news. She didn't disturb them. She went instead to the kitchen and picked up the phone.

'Sue. It's Mandy. Mandy Jones. Sorry to disturb you at home but I think you ought to pop round and check on Rose. Yes, now . . .'

Mandy paused, knowing how crazy it all sounded.

'Yes, I know she's out of hospital but . . . look, I've had a message from her. I can't tell you any more. Just check for me. Just this once. No, Mum doesn't know . . . Please, Sue. Er . . . yes, J'hon's doing fine . . . You will go, won't you?'

At eleven thirty the phone rang. A few minutes later Mrs Jones tapped on Mandy's door.

'You're still awake then?' she asked, without waiting for the obvious answer. 'That was Sue. She's just been round to see Rose.'

'And?' said Mandy, sitting up sharply.

'She's all right. Just a bit scared. Found her in the house alone. Babs came back, soon after. Said she'd only popped out for a minute to see her eldest daughter who lives round the corner. Daughter supported her story so . . .'

'She'd been out longer than a few minutes,' Mandy muttered. 'It was before ten when . . .'

'When what, Mandy? What's going on? You haven't been snooping round there instead of going to Taira's?'

'Don't be daft,' Mandy snapped. 'How could I? I don't even know the address.'

'Then how . . .'

'I had a tip-off from somebody and don't ask. I can't tell you. Not yet . . . soon . . . When I know what's going on myself,' she muttered, as her mother left the room.

Mandy glanced at the clock and groaned. Oh, well at least she could have a lie-in tomorrow and then she would have the rest of the weekend to work on J'hon with no distractions.

She began at eleven o'clock precisely the following morning, while her parents were at work.

'Right,' she said, shoving a piece of paper in front of J'hon. 'I want some answers. Where are you from?'

He picked up a pen and wrote a single word.

'Nowhere!' Mandy shrieked. 'Nowhere! Everyone's from somewhere, for heaven's sake. You mean you don't want to tell me.'

He nodded.

'Why? Are you in trouble?'

He nodded again.

'Serious trouble? Criminal stuff?'

More nods.

'Did you hurt someone?'

J'hon shook his head fiercely.

'Did you steal something?'

J'hon shrugged his shoulders.

'OK,' said Mandy, deciding to try a different route. 'You're pretty unusual, yes? You can't talk but . . . Why can't you talk? What happened to your tongue?'

Nothing, he wrote.

'Let me look.'

J'hon opened his mouth. His tongue was about half the normal length but looked fairly well formed.

'So you were born like that, I suppose. OK, you're not too good at language and stuff, so I guess you're not English. You say you've travelled a lot?'

He nodded enthusiastically.

'And you know a lot about maths and technology . . . so where does that come from?'

'Brain', J'hon wrote, before Mandy snatched the paper from him.

'OK, smart guy. I know it's your brain but other people have brains and they can't dismantle and remake Gameboys or read minds or . . . Look,' she said, as a thought struck her, 'I'm not going crazy, am I? I mean I'm not imagining all this? You can do things, can't you? Stuff that other people . . .'

He nodded.

'But you won't tell me how or why?'

J'hon screwed up his face as if in pain.

'Won't tell . . . or can't tell . . .' Mandy mused. 'Are you afraid?'

More nods.

'Of me?'

Vigorous head shaking.

'But you don't trust me?'

J'hon stood up and slowly turned his back on her. Mandy was hurt but not surprised. These kids who drifted in and out of her life trusted no-one. They'd been let down too many times and she guessed that J'hon was no exception. For the moment, she would get no further.

She flopped back in her chair, mulling over what little she knew, searching for rational explanations. Her mind refused to co-operate. It bounced around like a crazy pinball machine, touching on images of other kids they had fostered, articles she had read, programmes she had seen, disconnected jigsaw fragments which finally settled into a complete picture. A picture of Dustin Hoffman.

Mandy ran her hand through her hair. Why the heck was she thinking about Dustin Hoffman? An actor. Her dad's favourite. He was forever bringing home Hoffman films from the video shop. Some, like 'The Graduate', laughably outdated. 'Tootsie' was good fun though. Hoffman had played a woman in that. Or was it a man pretending to be a woman? He was brilliant anyway. One of the best character actors ever, her dad said. There was that amazing film with Tom Cruise . . . what was it called? Where Hoffman played a . . . That was it!

Mandy stood up and looked at J'hon who was staring blankly out of the kitchen window. Memories of the film came racing back. It was called 'Rainman'. About a young bloke and his older brother who was autistic. Mandy didn't know much about autism but she remembered Hoffman in the role, convincing as ever. Mathematical genius, brilliant with money, yet unable to communicate. Locked inside a private world, impossible for an outsider to understand. Clever but withdrawn, sensitive yet remote . . .

By the time Mandy's mother came home from work, Mandy was able to announce her latest theory. J'hon was autistic.

CHAPTER SEVEN

'It's possible,' Mandy's mother said. 'I don't know where it gets us, but it's possible. On the other hand . . .'

'What?'

'If he was autistic, you'd think he'd have been reported missing by now . . . by his parents . . . or a home . . . but there's absolutely nobody fitting J'hon's description on police files. Which reminds me, your circus connection might still turn up something. Nobody's confessed to anything yet but apparently there was some bother on the last night in Bradford. Group of Polish acrobats quit after some sort of fight. Haven't been seen since. Two of them were teenage males so . . .'

'Great,' said Mandy. 'So J'hon's probably an autistic, Polish acrobat drug addict with a touch of amnesia!'

She didn't say anything about J'hon's

fears or mention of criminal activity. But it would fit. Sort of. As much as anything seemed to fit.

For the time being, she judged it was best if J'hon kept a low profile and decided against taking him to the ice-rink. She took him instead to see Gran, who was still in hospital, recovering from her hip operation. Mandy spent as much time as she could with J'hon over the weekend, watching, probing, prying – getting nowhere. Almost nowhere. By Monday she had, at least, decided that her earlier fears about drugs were unfounded. He showed none of the classic symptoms she had come to recognize and even his bizarre behaviour seemed to have settled. Only in the matter of dress did he refuse to co-operate.

'Couldn't you leave the jewellery off?' Mandy's mother asked. 'Just for school?'

'And the gloves,' Mandy added. 'I don't know how you can wear those things day and night. Don't you ever take them off? Is there something wrong with your hands?'

J'hon looked bewildered by the barrage of questions and his gloved hands clutched the silver bangle. Keeping a low profile at school was going to be difficult, especially as J'hon had already attracted considerable attention. Jill wasn't the only girl to find him attractive and his popularity with the boys had increased dramatically after the first games lesson.

On Monday evening the boys persuaded J'hon to go to football practice where his immaculate ball skills combined with absolutely no knowledge of the rules caused a near riot. On Tuesday lunch time, Taira took him to chess club, told him the basics of the game and watched him beat seven people in rapid succession, including the teacher in charge. By Wednesday, Mandy was exhausted.

'What am I supposed to tell everybody?' she said as they walked through the playground on Wednesday evening. 'I'm sick of hearing questions I can't answer. I don't know who you are or where you're from. You don't talk, can hardly write and then this lunch time you calmly walk into the computer room and mend one of the machines Mrs O'Brien's been fiddling with for weeks. What am I supposed to tell . . . J'hon, are you paying any attention at all here, or am I wasting my time as usual?'

His head had flopped to the left, in his listening pose but as she was standing to his right, he clearly wasn't listening to her and, as far as she could see, there was no-one else within range.

'J'hon?' she yelled at him. 'This is serious. How can I help you if . . . oh, this is hopeless. You're not even trying to communicate. I wish you'd never . . . J'hon? What's going on? What are you looking at?'

His head was now upright. His colourful eyes, darting from side to side, searching. His gloved hands rubbing together, every part of his body tense and agitated.

'J'hon, I'm sorry. I didn't mean to upset you . . . I . . . J'hon? Where are you going? Come back. Don't be stupid. I didn't mean . . .'

Mandy stood, watching helplessly, as J'hon bolted out of the playground. She followed only as far as the gate. Pointless to carry on. He was far too quick. There was no way she could catch up. She'd talk to him at home. But he clearly wasn't intending to go home just yet. At the bottom of the road, he swung sharp right.

'Something wrong?'

Mandy turned at the sound of Jill's voice.

'Me,' she said. 'That's what's wrong. Me!'

In another playground, in a primary school on the other side of the city, a little girl stood, quite alone. Babs was late. She was always late, now. Sometimes she didn't come at all. The first time Rose had cried. The second time, her teacher had found her and given her a lift home. There had been a row.

'For 'eaven's sake, Rose,' Babs had said. 'Don't go bleating to them teachers over every little thing or they'll 'ave yer taken away. Yer six now. Surely yer can find yer own way home if I can't get there. I get there most days, don't I? It's just that sometimes . . . I get so tired, Rose. I fall asleep. It's them pills the doctor gave me for me 'eadaches, I reckon. I take 'em after lunch and the next thing I know, it's gone four o'clock. But yer all right. Yer can manage.

Yer a clever kid and yer know the way, don't yer?'

Rose knew the way but she didn't like walking home alone. There were busy roads to cross and once a big dog had barked at her. She'd had this funny feeling too. A feeling that someone was watching her. Following her, each time she made the journey alone. So she waited. Hovering in the corner, by the side gate, so her teacher wouldn't see. In her hand, she clutched her reading book with the card inside which said how well she was doing. She was supposed to read it to someone at home, like she used to with Mandy. But Babs had said she couldn't get on with books, so Rose read it to herself at night when the house was empty and she couldn't get to sleep. Lucky the book was inside a plastic bag. It had started to rain.

Rose pulled up the hood of her jacket. The one Mandy's mum had bought her before . . . It was no good thinking about it. It would only make her cry. Then Babs would be cross. She always got cross when Rose cried. Instead Rose blinked and counted the cars which passed along the narrow street. Two red ones. A blue one. Nothing for a while. An old man on a bike. A green van. Dirty. Sort of old-looking. Slowing down. Stopping by the gate. Rose stepped out to get a closer look. It could be Uncle Joe. He fixed cars. Came to pick her up sometimes in cars he was fixing.

But it was not Uncle Joe who got out. It was a younger man. Much younger. Brown hair flopping loose on his shoulders.

'Hi,' he said.

'No,' said Rose.

'No, what?' said the man smiling.

'No . . . thank you,' said Rose. 'I don't want to talk to you.'

She started to move off, quickly, down the road. She knew what to do. A police lady had come into school and told them. She had given them a bookmark with the words 'Say No to Strangers' printed on it.

'And never go anywhere with anyone you don't know,' Mandy's mother had told her.

'Run off,' Mandy had said. 'Scream if they pester you.'

Rose screamed and dropped her book, as the man grabbed her arm. His hand clamped over her mouth as he dragged her backwards, flinging open the rear door of the van. He lifted her and threw her inside, where someone else was waiting.

'It's my fault,' said Mandy pacing up and down the kitchen.

'No,' said her mother firmly.

'I shouldn't have gone on at him like that. I know what these kids are like. Push 'em too far and . . .'

'He's probably just walking round somewhere. He's a big boy, Mandy. He can take care of himself. Give him an hour or so and he'll be back.'

'It's two hours already! Mum, I think we ought to . . .'

Mandy's speech was halted by the sound of the doorbell.

'He's back!' she yelled, tripping over Meg in her race to the door.

But it was not J'hon who stood on the doorstep.

'What is it?' said Mandy, staring at Sue

and the two men who stood beside her. 'What's happened to him?'

'Him?' said Sue.

'J'hon.'

'Er – nothing as far as I know. Isn't he home? Look, I think we'd better come in.'

Mandy had known the men were police officers, even before Sue introduced them. No uniforms, but Mandy had had enough dealings with the police to know.

Accepting tea, they sat round the kitchen table, grim-faced.

'It's Rose,' said Sue, breaking the silence. 'We think she might have been kidnapped.'

'Kidnapped,' Mandy screamed. 'Who . . . why . . . how do you know? What . . .'

'Calmly,' said one of the police officers. 'Sombody saw it happen. An old lady whose house overlooks Rose's school saw a kid being bundled into a van. She's house-bound and on her own, so she couldn't do much except phone us. We thought she was mistaken at first. No kids had been reported missing. Then Miss Jenson got in touch with us.'

'I'd popped round to see Rose,' Sue explained. 'I'd been a bit worried about her with that fall business and everything. Anyway, she wasn't home. Babs didn't have a clue where she was. Didn't even think it was strange she hadn't turned up. Said she'd be out playing somewhere. But I couldn't see her in the street and I know Rose. She's a reliable sort of kid. Not one to wander.'

'But,' said Mandy, desperately, 'that doesn't mean anything. It might not have been Rose . . .'

'Fits the old woman's description, I'm afraid,' said the other police officer. 'Gave us a good description of the van too. No registration number, though, unfortunately. She also got a good look at the young man responsible. Thinks she could identify him. You say this lad J'hon isn't home?'

'Now, wait a minute,' said Mandy's mother. 'Surely you don't think J'hon . . .'

'We don't think anything at the moment,' said the officer. 'But the description rang a bell with Miss Jenson. Thought it sounded very like the boy you'd taken on. Probably isn't. Our witness said the guy was in his twenties. But then, old people can get confused about age. Anyway, we'd like to have a quick word with your lad, if only to eliminate him. To be frank, I've got a far more likely character in mind but we have to check out every possibility.'

Mandy's head had sunk into her hands. Rose missing. J'hon missing. He had seemed to know such a lot about her. But how? Who was he? What was his connection with Rose? Should she tell the police? But what was there to tell? It all sounded so crazy. Maybe that was it. Maybe J'hon was crazy. Really crazy.

Someone shook her shoulder. She looked up, realizing her mother had been speaking to her.

'So I'm going to have a drive round with Sue,' she said. 'See if we can find him. Sue'll drop me off at your dad's office. He can drive me home. Now if J'hon turns up, you phone this number and ask for Detective Super . . .'

'But, Mum . . .'

'I know, Mandy,' said Mrs Jones. 'I don't

think J'hon's got anything to do with this either but we've got to be sure. OK?'

Mandy nodded.

'And you'll be all right? I won't be more than an hour.'

Mandy closed the door behind them and stood at the window watching them all drive away. Then she flopped onto the floor, crying. Meg ambled over, nuzzled her nose into Mandy's face and began to whine in sympathy.

They were still curled up together, almost asleep, ten minutes later when J'hon arrived.

He had let himself in, quietly, through the back door and stood, hovering over them until Meg, sensing his presence, got up, wagging her tail.

Mandy leapt to her feet.

'Where have you been?' she yelled. 'What's going on? What have you done?'

J'hon shuffled nervously, his gloved hand tightly clutching a book in a plastic wallet.

'What's that?' said Mandy, snatching it from him.

She pulled the book from the wallet and stared at the card inside. Reading Record – Rose Hutchins, 2B. Next to it was a bookmark with the words 'Say No to Strangers' printed on it.

CHAPTER EIGHT

Mandy pushed past J'hon and went towards the kitchen. No time to talk. No time for explanations. What had her mother said? Phone the police if he comes back. And he was back all right. With Rose's schoolbook. What more evidence did she want? What was she waiting for? And yet – somehow, she couldn't believe it. Weird he might be, but he wouldn't hurt anybody. Would he? She was in the house with him, all alone. What if he was dangerous? Insane, even.

Mandy shook her head in denial and then doubled over as a pain ripped through her stomach. This was always her weak spot, when she got nervous. Mandy dashed towards the stairs and the toilet. The phone call would have to wait.

When she emerged, the phone was

ringing. She rushed downstairs and picked it up.

'Mrs Henderson?' Mandy said, somewhat surprised.

She had been expecting her mother or the police. Anybody but their neighbour who hadn't spoken to them for eighteen months.

'You're worried about your privets?' said Mandy, bemused. 'Well, that was a long time ago. Lucy's not here any more and Dad paid for . . . What? You can see out of your bathroom window . . . Mum's car . . . bonnet up . . . oh, my . . .'

Mandy slammed the phone down and ran outside. Mum had gone with Sue, so her car should be in the garage. But it wasn't. It was out on the narrow street at the back of their house. The engine was running . . . how had he . . . Mum always kept the keys in her handbag . . . Mandy pushed past Meg who was standing by the back gate, wagging her tail.

J'hon was putting the car into gear. It jerked forward. He was a lunatic. Definitely unstable, like Lucy had been. He might be clever but . . .

He looked confused as he saw her out of the rear-view mirror, frantically waving her arms. He reversed. Far too quickly. Mandy stepped out of the way. There was a thud. Mandy dropped to her knees beside the dog, glancing back at the open gate. She had left the gate open. Meg had got out. It was her fault.

No. Not her fault. All her anger suddenly turned on J'hon who was standing beside her.

'Look what you've done!' she screamed at him. 'Look what you've done now. She's dying. She's dying.'

Blood trickled from the side of Meg's mouth. Vet. She'd have to phone a vet. It was too late. She knew that. But she had to do something. She couldn't just kneel here, sobbing, watching Meg die.

Mandy stood up at the same time that J'hon dropped to his knees.

'What are you doing? Leave her alone.'

J'hon pulled off his gloves and threw them at Mandy. She stooped, automatically, to retrieve them from where they had fallen at her feet. She couldn't stand up immediately. She felt dizzy, as if she were going to faint. She took a few deep breaths, pressed her hands on the ground and tried to stand. It was then that she saw the nails. J'hon's nails were long, perfectly manicured and orange. Bright orange. And they were growing. The nails were growing as she watched. Not normal growth. They were twisting. Contorting into different shapes. One was flat, sharp-edged, like a knife. Another tubular, a third, thin and pointed, like a needle.

Mandy gripped the base of the gatepost, leant forward and was sick, as she watched the needle plunge into Meg's neck.

Mandy didn't know how long she crouched there, watching the bizarre operation. Or even whether she was there at all. It had the hazy, unreal quality of a nightmare. She wanted to scream or cry out but her vocal cords, like the rest of her body, failed her. Her legs wouldn't move. Her arms flopped limp at her side and her eyes swam in and out of focus as she tried to concentrate on J'hon's clever little nails.

She was still propped against the gate-post when Meg got up and ambled past her as though nothing was wrong. J'hon, his silky gloves back in place, took hold of Mandy's arm. Her last image before she fainted was of Meg chasing birds in the garden. Tired, old Meg hadn't done that for years.

When Mandy came round, she was lying on the settee in the lounge with a cup of tea on the table in front of her. J'hon must have carried her inside. He sat now on the chair opposite, smiling uncertainly, as people do when their well-meaning actions backfire.

'Who are you?' she managed to say before her eyes closed again.

She felt the glove stroking her eyelid. J'hon was sitting beside her now. It had been a dream, of course. All of it. Rose, J'hon, Meg – a crazy dream.

'Take your gloves off,' she murmured.

J'hon shook his head.

'Take them off!' she yelled.

Slowly, he began to pull the glove from his left hand. Mandy watched as his slender fingers were revealed. Dark fingers with slightly discoloured nails. Reddish brown, as though they'd been trapped in a door and badly bruised. Not bright orange, as she'd remembered and certainly not extraordinary in length.

'Other hand,' she demanded.

The right glove came off. Five more normal, if discoloured, nails.

'I thought . . . I mean, I saw . . . Meg . . . your nails . . .'

Mandy paused, wondering exactly who was going crazy. J'hon's strange behaviour, Rose's disappearance – it was enough to unnerve anybody. To make her start imagining things and yet . . .

'I want to know about Rose, J'hon,' she said, suddenly able to focus her mind on what was really important. 'What have you done to Rose?'

She instinctively pressed back as J'hon stretched out his hands towards her.

'Paper,' she said. 'Paper. We need a pen and some paper.'

He shook his head, replaced his gloves and smiled.

'Don't smile. Don't! This is serious, J'hon. I've got to know. I've got to know what's . . .'

He grabbed her hands and pulled her into a sitting position. Then he let go, stretched out his gloved hands and placed a finger in each of his ears.

'Uh?' Mandy groaned.

He removed his fingers and pointed to her.

'Uh?' said Mandy, again. 'You want me to put my fingers in my ears like you did? No . . . er . . . you want . . . oh, no! You're not sticking your talons in my ears. Gloves or no gloves. No way! I don't care what you did for Meg, out there. You're not touching me.'

J'hon ignored her protests. He leant forward and pressed his fingers into Mandy's ears. There was an immediate burst of sound, like turning on a Walkman at full volume. But this Walkman had pictures too. A TV screen switched on inside her mind and the film showing was definitely science fiction. Fast. Moving far too fast for her to understand.

Mandy gasped. She had never understood before the expression to take one's breath away. But what she was witnessing did exactly that. J'hon, sensing her discomfort, removed his fingers, allowing her to breathe slow, deep gulps of air.

'Those images?' she whispered, at last. 'Those distances . . . those incredible distances. What are you saying? Are you telling me you come from . . . oh, no . . . it isn't possible . . . you're lying . . . you . . .'

The probing fingers made contact again and, suddenly, Mandy knew. This was no lie. Bizarre. Improbable. The working of a deranged mind or an overactive imagination, possibly. But not a lie. Before she could get to grips with any of it, the images of endless space faded, replaced by something more tangible and much more important. A little girl, lying on a bed in an otherwise empty room.

'Rose. You know where she is?'

J'hon removed his fingers and nodded.

'Why, J'hon, why? Why have you taken Rose? What's she . . .'

The vigorous shaking of J'hon's head stopped her.

'Not you,' she said. 'Someone else. Someone else has taken Rose? But you knew. That's why you ran off earlier. That's why you tried to take the car . . .'

J'hon nodded continually as she spoke.

'But you're not directly involved, right? Promise me, J'hon. Swear you're not . . .'

His hurt expression was enough.

'So you found the book. Yes? Rose must have dropped it when . . . J'hon,' she said, clutching his arm. 'We've got to phone the police. Tell them.'

J'hon shook his head.

'Why not?'

She didn't need an answer. It was all too obvious. What could they say? How could they explain how J'hon knew? No-one was going to believe this. She wasn't sure she believed it herself. Whatever the explanation for J'hon's amazing abilities, it was crazy. Seriously crazy. Not even her parents, or the social workers, could come to terms with J'hon. Let alone the police.

And if they did? What then? What would happen to J'hon? What would they do to him? Until she knew for certain who he was and why he was here, she couldn't put him at risk. He was frightened and confused, like all the kids they fostered. Only J'hon, she was beginning to suspect, was further away from home than most.

'OK,' she said. 'Just me. Can you take me to Rose?'

He nodded and pulled her to her feet. She went into the kitchen, hastily scribbled a note, hid Rose's schoolbook in a drawer under a pile of tea towels and grabbed her jacket. She called Meg in from the garden. The dog bounded past, wagging her tail, her eyes bright, almost youthful again. Whatever J'hon had done, it was powerful stuff.

Outside, J'hon headed towards the car.

'No,' said Mandy. 'I don't care what you can do with your clever little nails, it's too dangerous. You don't know the first thing about driving. We'll have to walk or get a bus or . . . Wait a minute . . .'

Mandy rummaged in her purse.

'Taxi. If we get a taxi from the town centre, could you direct it? OK. Good. Come on.'

Mandy was glad she had her skating lesson money as the taxi crossed the city and drove out the other side. It looked as though she would need it.

'Left,' Mandy screamed at the driver as she noticed J'hon point.

'Can't you give me more notice?' the driver yelled, as car horns beeped. 'I was in the wrong lane then.'

'I'm sorry,' said Mandy. 'My friend can't speak. So I don't know in advance.'

'Blasted kids,' the driver muttered.

'Are you sure this is right, J'hon?' Mandy said, as the taxi weaved its way through a vast estate.

It was one of the council estates with a reputation for crime and crumbling buildings. Council and tenants had got together in an attempt to tidy it up. They had already driven through the revamped section. Now they were in a derelict area, probably scheduled for total redevelopment. Houses were boarded-up, gardens overgrown with weeds, pavements cracked and strewn with debris.

'Stop,' Mandy instructed the driver, as J'hon held up his hand.

'What you kids up to?' the driver asked, as he took Mandy's money.

'Survey,' said Mandy hastily. 'For social studies at school. About urban renewal.'

'Don't see why they can't teach you something proper,' said the driver, as he left them standing in the middle of an empty street.

Mrs Jones hovered by the back door and stared at the car.

'I can't understand what it's doing out,' she said following her husband into the kitchen. 'I'm sure I put it away.'

'You can't have done, Cath. Hardly surprising if you forgot with all this going on.'

'I know. Even the dog's acting strange. Get down, Meg. She's like a puppy! Get down. Go find Mandy.'

As she issued the order, she saw the note on the table.

'What's this supposed to mean? "J'hon's safe. I've had to go out. I'm fine. Love, Mandy."'

'I thought she was supposed to phone the police if J'hon turned up?'

'She was but I might have known this would happen. She doesn't think J'hon's involved.'

'Do you?'

'No. He happens to vaguely fit that old woman's description but then so would hundreds of others. Even so, we don't really know anything about him, do we? And Mandy was convinced he knew Rose somehow. Oh, I don't know. I thought Mandy had more sense. I think we ought to phone . . .'

As she said the word, the phone rang. Mrs Jones picked it up, while her husband paced up and down the kitchen, unable to glean anything from her short replies of yes and no. Only when she started to talk about Mandy's disappearance, did he begin to guess.

'The police?' he said, as she replaced the receiver.

She nodded.

'They know what's happened to Rose,' she said. 'They don't know where she is, but they reckon they know who's got her and why.'

CHAPTER NINE

'Is this the street?' Mandy asked.

J'hon shook his head and took hold of her hand. Of course, he wouldn't have led the taxi straight to the place. They'd have to be careful. Very careful.

'Do you know who it is, J'hon? Do you know who's got Rose?'

He shook his head.

'Is she hurt? Has he hurt her?'

J'hon shook his head again.

He had led her along the street, round the back of some houses and into an alleyway. Mandy looked at her watch. Quarter past seven. It would be getting dark soon. She shivered. It was none too warm either, with a light drizzle starting to fall. She pulled up her jacket collar as J'hon stopped and pointed towards the end of the alley where a tower block loomed, grim and unfriendly.

'In there? She's being held in there?'

J'hon nodded.

'Is she alone?'

He shrugged.

'You don't know? Could you tell, if we got closer?'

He nodded again.

They moved quickly through the alley but before they reached the end, their exit was blocked. Three youths, a little older than themselves, stood at the end.

'Is it them?' Mandy whispered. 'Are they anything to do with . . .'

J'hon shook his head, squeezed her hand and turned slowly to lead her back the other way.

'Hey!' one of the youths shouted. 'You. Pretty boy. Stay where you are.'

J'hon carried on walking, clutching Mandy's trembling hand. The other end of the alley was blocked by two more youths. The five boys closed in until Mandy and J'hon were surrounded.

'You aren't from round 'ere,' said one with ginger hair. 'What yer doing?'

'We . . . er . . .' Mandy began.

She could hardly tell this lot they were doing a survey for school and she certainly wasn't going to tell them the truth.

'I weren't talkin' to you,' said the lad. 'I was talkin' to him. Him with the fancy gear.'

'He can't answer you,' said Mandy, hurriedly. 'He can't speak.'

'What's the matter? Cat got his tongue?' the boy said, as his mates grinned approval at such wit.

'Thing is,' said a boy with three gold studs in his nose. 'We don't like strangers prowlin' around, see? And he looks right strange ter me.'

The boys laughed again.

'So y'ed better f—'

'Language, Baz,' said the one with ginger hair, who seemed to be the leader. 'Not in front of a lady. Right? What Baz means is that you ought ter leave. Right?'

'OK,' said Mandy. 'We're going.'

'Thing is,' said Baz. 'It aren't so easy. Shall I tell 'em, Nick?'

The ginger-haired one nodded.

'Yer see, there's a charge for usin' this alley.'

'Charge?' Mandy repeated.

'Bright, aren't yer?' said Baz. 'Costs extra if yer a smart a—'

'Language, Baz. What've I told yer?'

Mandy stared at them, her hopes fading. What had they got themselves into? They'd been crazy to come alone. All this time they were wasting, Rose could be . . .

'So hand it over.'

'What?' said Mandy. 'All I've got left is one pound fifty.'

She was about to open her bag but J'hon grabbed her arm to stop her.

'We've got to give them something, J'hon. I've got the money and . . .'

'His jewellery,' said Nick. 'The watch and the bangle and that fancy belt. We'll take them.'

Mandy felt J'hon's grip on her arm tighten. What was he going to do? He never took that stuff off. Never. Still gripping Mandy with his left arm, he pulled her close to him and stretched out his right hand as if inviting them to take the bangle.

113

'Get it, Baz,' said Nick.

Baz sauntered forward and grabbed J'hon's wrist.

'Move it,' Nick ordered.

'Doesn't seem to 'ave a catch,' Baz muttered.

He glared menacingly at J'hon, his face up close. He opened his mouth as if to speak but instead he reeled backwards, clutching his chest.

'Quit muckin' about, Baz. You! Pretty boy. Get those things off. Throw 'em over 'ere.'

J'hon looked at Nick and smiled.

'So yer think it's funny. I'll show . . . '

He didn't get any further. His hands went up to his throat as he writhed about, apparently trying to throttle himself.

'Get him,' Baz shouted, still clutching his chest.

The third boy tried to advance but dropped to his knees after only one step. Nick, still performing his bizarre ritual, tripped over him and sprawled flat on the floor. J'hon swung round to face the other two but they had gone.

The nameless boy crawled along the alley on his hands and knees. Only when he got to the end did he stand and run. Nick and Baz, made of sterner stuff, somehow pulled themselves upright but they couldn't face J'hon for long.

'What's 'e doin'? Who the hell does he think he is?' Baz muttered, clutching his head. '—ing Superman.'

This time Nick didn't bother to correct the language. He screamed a few expletives of his own as he and Baz backed to the end of the alley, turned and ran.

Mandy leant against the wall, breathing deeply. She bent over and started to retch.

'I'm sorry,' she said. 'I always get this way when I'm nervous. My stomach sort of packs up on me.'

J'hon stroked her hair and before she knew what was happening he'd slipped an ungloved finger into the corner of her mouth. She felt a trickle of sweet liquid roll over her tongue and down her throat.

'Is there anything you can't do?' she asked as her rumbling stomach immediately stabilized.

J'hon nodded, touched his lips and smiled.

'Talk. You can't talk. You're a telepath, right? Is that why your tongue's like that? Shrivelled, like an appendix, 'cos you don't need it any more. Can you . . .'

Mandy stopped herself as J'hon nodded. There was so much she wanted to know. Needed to know. But there was Rose. For the moment, rescuing Rose was her priority. And with J'hon around maybe it wouldn't be as difficult as she thought.

Rose sat, tense and alert on the edge of the dirty mattress as she heard footsteps in the corridor. The men were coming. The bad men who had brought her here. Her thumb went into her mouth. Then she pulled it out again. Mandy had told her that big girls didn't do that. But maybe they did. Sometimes. When they were scared. The thumb went back in. It was better than screaming.

She had screamed at first. The minute they'd removed the tape which had bound her mouth. The men had laughed.

'Scream away, darlin',' the older one had said. 'Won't do no good. No-one can hear yer up here.'

And she had screamed. Long after they had gone. Screamed until she could force no more sound from her aching throat. Hammered on the locked door until her knuckles bled. Then she had cried. Not because the men had hurt her. They hadn't hurt her. Not really. Not yet.

She jumped up and pressed herself against the boarded-up window as the footsteps stopped and she heard the sound of a bolt being drawn back on the outside of the door. What was she supposed to do? She had listened to Mandy and to the police lady who had come into school. They had told her never to go with strangers. But what if they grabbed you? What if you didn't have any choice? No-one had said anything about that. What were you supposed to do when the bad men came back?

The door was flung open and Rose started to scream.

'Shut 'er up, can't yer?' said the older man, with the tattooed hands.

Rose stopped screaming as the long-haired man moved towards her. 'That's better,' said the older one. 'Thought you said there'd be no bother, Jimmy. Kid's supposed to know yer, aren't she?'

'Yer don't remember me, do yer, Rose? Yer don't remember yer Uncle Jimmy?'

Rose shook her head. There was Uncle Joe, at Babs's house. There were even three aunties who turned up sometimes with babies in pushchairs. But no Uncle Jimmy. Not that she remembered.

'How old was she when yer last saw 'er?' the other man asked.

'Dunno. About two, I reckon. But I've seen the photos 'er dad's got. It's Rose all right.'

'I'm not sayin' it aren't. But she 'asn't seen any photos of you, has she? So how's she supposed to recognize you, eh? Yer great cretin. Listen, kid. This is yer uncle, right? Yer Uncle Jimmy. Yer dad's brother. Yer remember yer dad, don't yer?'

Rose shook her head. She knew they didn't mean Alan, the man she had called Dad. He was Mandy's dad. Not hers. Babs had explained all that. They meant someone else. Someone before. Someone who had . . . She shook her head again.

As they headed towards the flats, Mandy could see they were as deserted as everything else in this grim neighbourhood. Windows were either broken or boarded-up. There were no lights, no curtains, no sign of life.

'You sure?' Mandy whispered, as they slipped inside. 'You sure this is it?'

It was dark and stank of stale beer and urine. Mandy experimented with a light switch. Nothing. No use trying the lifts then. She headed for the stairs. J'hon pulled her back, into the recess under them.

'What's wrong? Why can't we go up? Oh, this is hopeless. It's too dark to write messages and besides, I haven't got a pen. Can't we communicate? You're smart enough. Isn't there some way we can . . .'

J'hon's fingers stretched towards her head.

'Not that,' Mandy hissed. 'You nearly

blew my brains out, last time. It's too . . . fast. Too intense.'

J'hon let his hands drop and stood facing her, his eyes glowing and hypnotic.

'Is that more better?'

Mandy heard the question, clearly, though J'hon's lips remained closed. The voice in her head was soft, lyrical. He spoke like the French students who visited the school last year. More or less correctly. Stresses in the wrong places.

'How do you do that?' she asked.

'I do it all the time. It's you that have the problem. Now I see how limited your brain is . . .'

'Thanks very much!'

'I know I have to shout into your mind, very loud.'

'Like me, speaking up for Gran,' said Mandy, smiling, forgiving his insult. 'OK. Why can't we go up there?'

'Too dangerous. I can feel from here. People with her. Two people.'

'But then we've got to . . . she might be hurt . . . she . . .'

'No. Not hurt. I sense if hurt.'

'How?' said Mandy. 'How do you do all this stuff?'

'It is how I am. I read thoughts of those close by. Feelings of people further off. I sense Rose because you do.'

'But I don't,' said Mandy. 'I didn't know about her accident. I didn't know when . . .'

'Yes,' J'hon's thoughts interrupted. 'Yes you did. But you not know how to access deep thoughts – yet.'

'Yet?' said Mandy. 'You mean I could?'

'All your people could. You basically same as me. My people . . .'

'Your people?' said Mandy. 'All that stuff back at the house. What you were trying to tell me is . . .'

She paused, as if putting it into words would do nothing more than confirm her own insanity.

'You're . . . from . . . I mean the things you can do . . .'

'I think the word is alien,' said J'hon. 'You are trying to ask me whether I am an alien.'

'Are you?'

'I am different. I am not supposed to be here.'

'And is that your crime? Is that what you're scared of? Discovery by us or by . . .'

'Discovery, yes. People must not know the things I can do.'

'But those boys in the alley,' said Mandy. 'What if they tell someone?'

'I not think they will.'

'No. Maybe not but . . . what happened back there? How did you do that?'

'Very easy,' said J'hon. 'Very weak minds. Mine much stronger. I make them feel own aggression. Turn it against selves.'

'Oh, is that all?' said Mandy. 'You could rule the world if . . .'

'I not want to do that,' said J'hon, looking hurt. 'I mean no harm. Already I cause much trouble. I make for you much confusion.'

'You can say that again,' said Mandy, attempting a smile.

'I know. And I am sorry. It will not be for much more time. Soon I go. But first we find Rose, yes?'

CHAPTER TEN

'I don't remember. I don't remember,' Rose yelled. 'I don't remember him and I don't remember you.'

'OK,' said Jimmy, grabbing her shoulders. 'Don't start up again. Just take my word for it. I'm yer uncle, right? And I aren't gonna hurt yer. Not if yer a good girl, eh? Here, 'ave some chocolate.'

He let go of her trembling shoulders and pulled a bar of chocolate from his pocket. He had to get the kid on his side, somehow. He held it out to her. Rose looked at it. It was one of her favourites. And she was hungry. Very hungry.

'Suit yerself,' he said, as she shook her head.

'I blame the teachers,' said the other man. 'Fillin' their 'eads with rubbish about not takin' sweets from strangers. I keep tellin' yer, kid. We aren't strangers. He's yer uncle and I'm . . . well . . . I'm a sorta mate of yer dad's. Yer can call me . . . er . . . Pete. Yeah, just Pete. That'll do. Now stop being stupid and eat the bloody chocolate. We're just lookin' after yer fer a bit, OK?'

He grabbed the chocolate from Jimmy, took the wrapper off and thrust it into her hand.

'Eat it,' he ordered. 'It aren't poisoned or nowt. Yer'd be no good to us dead. Least not yet.'

'Shut it, Pete,' Jimmy said. 'Yer frightening 'er. Nothin's gonna happen to yer, Rose. Not if your dad tells us where the stuff is. And he will. I mean, I know what he's like. Fouled things up for me, good and proper, he did. But he's got a soft spot for you. Once we can get a message to 'im. Once he knows we've got yer. He'll tell us all right. He misses you, yer know. Oh, I know he used to get mad when he'd 'ad a drink or two. But he never meant to 'urt yer. He's always goin' on about yer is our Sammy.'

Sammy. Rose didn't know what they were talking about. What they meant. But she knew that name. Not Sam, like that kid

at school. Or Samuel like Mandy's neighbour. Sammy. Oh yes, she knew it all right.
Last time she'd heard it someone had been
screaming. Screaming the name over and
over. Pictures swarmed into Rose's mind
as she battled to shut them out. A half
open door. Table legs. Bits of food and cat
hairs on the floor. High-heeled shoes. Man
yelling. Lady screaming . . .

J'hon's head tilted to one side.

'What's wrong?' said Mandy. 'What's
happening? Are they hurting her?'

'Not hurting. But . . .'

'What?' Mandy screamed, as J'hon
clamped his hand over her mouth.

'Her pain come from inside. Men somehow make bad memories for her. Is this
true?' said J'hon removing his hand.

'Is what true?' said Mandy, in the quietest
voice she could manage.

'Can't you see it? Feel it?'

'No,' said Mandy, almost screaming again
with frustration.

'Her mother. She's seeing her die.'

'No. That's not possible,' said Mandy.

'She was barely three . . . she was upstairs, asleep. She knows what happened. She's been told. But she never talks about it. She doesn't remember. She didn't see it. She wasn't there.'

'You people,' said J'hon, holding her hand. 'You bury your deep thoughts. Deep feelings. To understand, you must let yourself feel what others feel. See what they see. Know what they know. Then to have wars is impossible. To kill impossible.'

'But we'd all go mad,' said Mandy, 'if we could feel each other's pain.'

'No,' said J'hon, smiling. 'But perhaps you have a long way to go. Before you can accept the pain of others you must learn to accept own pain. You people fight it. Make pretend it never happened, as Rose has done.'

Mandy opened her mouth to argue and closed it again. He was right. All the kids that had stayed with them, they had all blocked things out. Things in their lives they couldn't face. She had done it herself, when Grandad died. Refused to go to the funeral. Stood by his empty chair and spoken to him. Screamed at Gran when she'd given away his clothes. On the day of the ice-skating show, she'd looked for him in the audience, intending to wave as she always did. Then she had broken down and cried. Right there in the middle of the rink.

How did J'hon do it? How could he feel like that and not go mad? Compassion. Understanding. They were possible. But total empathy? If she had felt the hurt of every child who had stayed with them, every victim of war, or famine . . . Rose. If she could feel what Rose was feeling now . . . or Mum. How long had they been gone? She'd be frantic.

'J'hon, we've got to do something. Now. Before it's too late.'

'Sssh . . . someone's listening.'

'There can't be,' Mandy hissed. 'No-one could have come through the door or down the stairs without us hearing them.'

'I make my thoughts too powerful. Some-one's listening,' J'hon said again.

Then he was silent.

Mandy could get no more out of him

except irritating nods and shakes of the head. He was insistent they could do nothing until the men came down, as they surely would. If they moved now, someone might get hurt and, for the moment, Rose was in no real danger.

No danger. It was all right for J'hon to say that, Mandy thought bitterly, as she left the recess and stared round the deserted hall. A door to one of the ground floor flats lay open. Beside it was a sign which had been half torn from the wall. She moved closer and peered at it. Court. The flats were called something Court. Not that it helped. She wondered if she should go outside. Try to find a phone. Contact her mother, the police, anyone. But there was unlikely to be a phone in working order in reasonable distance and besides, those boys might still be lurking.

Suddenly J'hon was standing beside her, staring at the broken sign, his gloved hands pressed against his temples.

'Something wrong?' she hissed.

He shook his head.

'You'd tell me if . . .'

He nodded. Suddenly his voice was inside her head again.

'I have to leave. Very soon now. So I send message for help.'

'Message? Who to?'

'To your mother.'

'How? There's no phone.'

'Never mind that,' said J'hon. 'You get your wish. It is time to act.'

Sue Jenson sat down on the sofa next to Mrs Jones whilst Alan Jones paced up and down behind them. In the kitchen, two police officers sat sifting through information about Rose. They had come round shortly after the phone call.

'Right,' Detective Superintendent Callaghan had said, briskly. 'We're pretty sure she's with Jimmy Hutchins.'

'Quick work,' Mandy's mother said. 'How did you . . . ?'

'Babs phoned us. She got a message from him. He just said not to worry, he was looking after Rose for a bit. She wouldn't come to any harm and she'd be back soon. Oh, and not to bother calling the police.'

'She probably wouldn't have done either,' said Sue, 'if we hadn't already known Rose was missing.'

'Oh, I don't know,' Callaghan had answered, thoughtfully. 'I think she probably hates the Hutchins clan more than she hates us.'

'So why?' Mr Jones had asked. 'What's Jimmy up to?'

'I've got a few ideas,' said Callaghan. 'I got some checks done, as soon as I heard that old woman's description. Sounded just like our Jimmy. Only I thought he was still inside for that robbery a few years back. Remember that, Sue?'

'Sure. Pretty nasty. Big house. Old couple. Left tied up in a cellar overnight. The lady died of a stroke a few months later, didn't she?'

'Yes. But we couldn't prove her death was a direct result of the burglary. So Jimmy and Pete Eddison got a pretty light sentence, in my opinion.'

'And Sammy got off completely, right?' Sue added.

'Right,' Callaghan had said. 'We didn't

have enough evidence against him and the other two weren't saying anything. It suited them to have Sammy on the outside. We only ever recovered a fraction of the stuff. I reckon Sammy's still got the rest. Couldn't ever get anything out of him, though. And then, of course, he blew it. Got put away himself for murdering his wife.'

'And now,' Sue said, 'Jimmy and Pete are out, with Sammy stuck inside for a fair bit longer.'

'And,' said Callaghan, 'what's interesting is the prison governor tells me there'd been a lot of aggro shortly before Jimmy's release. Had to put Jimmy and Sammy in different wings. So I guess Sammy's not letting on where the stuff is and Jimmy's trying to put the pressure on. He's daft enough. If I'm right, sooner or later some-one'll turn up one visiting time to break the news to Sammy. And when that happens, we'll be waiting. But until then, we'll do it the hard way. Search the files. See if we can come up with some clues as to where they might be.'

'Can't Babs help with that?' Mr Jones had asked.

'No,' said Callaghan. 'Not a hope. She went completely hysterical on us when we tried to question her. Seemed to think we were blaming her. Had to get a doctor in to sedate her, in the end. So, we're on our own now. I'm banking on the fact that they're still in the city . . .'

They could be anywhere, Mrs Jones thought, as she mulled over Callaghan's words. So, for that matter, could Mandy.

'Why hasn't she phoned?' she said out loud.

'Still no word?' Sue asked.

Cath shook her head and stared at Sue. She looked pale and agitated. Unusual for Sue, normally so professional and in control.

'She'll be all right,' Sue said. 'Can't understand why they took off like that, though. J'hon wasn't involved.'

'Not with this,' said Cath. 'But who knows? Maybe he's got something else to hide. That's why he wasn't too keen to wait around for the police. How can we be sure he didn't force Mandy to write that note? If she was OK she'd have contacted me by now. I know she would . . . I . . .'

Cath let her head slump forward into her hands and began to rub her eyes.

'Headache?' Sue asked. 'Can I get you an aspirin or . . .'

'No,' said Cath. 'It's not a headache. It's a picture. I think I'm going mad. What with Rose and now Mandy . . .'

'Picture?' said Sue, urgently. 'What sort of picture?'

'Oh, it's nothing . . . well, yes it is. Like a dream. A recurring dream. Only more vivid. I keep seeing a block of flats. A tower block. Deserted. Derelict. I'm sorry,' she said, her eyes appealing to both her husband and Sue. 'I don't usually . . . I mean, I know you'll think I'm crazy.'

'No,' said Sue, drawing the word out slowly. 'Or, if you are, we both are . . . I've been seeing it, too.'

'What does it mean?' said Cath.

'It means,' said her husband, firmly, 'that we're all under a lot of pressure, nothing more. Nothing less.'

'I'm always under pressure,' Sue snapped. 'It's my job to handle pressure. And I don't go around seeing things.'

'The same thing,' Cath mused. 'That's what makes it so odd. We're both seeing the same thing. I think we ought to . . .'

'Oh, no,' said Alan, as his wife and Sue headed towards the kitchen. 'Tell the police that and they'll have you booked into the nearest asylum.'

Detective Superintendent Callaghan made no mention of asylums or madness. He listened without a trace of a smile, or even worse, a sneer.

'And you say it's called something Court?'

'Yes,' said the two women together.

'Nothing else?'

'No, sorry.'

'But this is ridiculous,' said Alan Jones, hovering in the doorway.

'Maybe,' said Callaghan, glancing at his junior officer, whose sceptical eyes dropped immediately to his paperwork. 'But a psychic once located a serial killer for me, when we'd abandoned all hope of catching him, so these days I'm pretty open-minded. Especially when we have absolutely nothing else to go on. Now, do any of you remember the Hutchins family living at an address of that sort?'

Sue shook her head. She had been involved with Rose Hutchins virtually since her birth. There were records on the family stretching back three generations. Sammy himself had been in and out of care since he was five years old. He had lived in so many places. Moved so many times.

'It would be in there, somewhere,' she said, pointing to the documents which littered the table.

'Take a look at this,' said the young officer, hesitantly holding up a piece of paper. 'I think I might have something.'

CHAPTER ELEVEN

'No,' Rose yelled. 'I won't. I won't listen. I don't want to. I don't want to see. You can't make me. Stop it. Stop it.'

She flung the half-eaten chocolate on the floor.

'What's she on about?' said Pete. 'We're not doin' owt. All we want is what's ours. It might take a while that's all. But once we can get a message to yer dad . . .'

'He's not my dad. Stop it. I hate him. I hate you. I want Mandy. Mandy. Mandy. Mandy. Tell them to stop it.'

'Who the hell's Mandy?' Pete said.

'I dunno,' said Jimmy. 'She were with this family before she went back to her gran. Is that who it is? Did yer live with Mandy, Rose?'

'I want her. I want her,' Rose yelled.

'Bloody kid's 'avin' a fit,' Pete snarled as Rose hurled herself at the far wall. 'What we gonna do, Jimmy? Yer said this'd be easy. Win the kid round. Get the stuff from Sammy. Disappear. Let the kid go. Get 'er ter say we were just lookin' after 'er for a bit, if there were any bother. Not a chance, Jimmy! The minute we let 'er go, we'll be back inside. An' I wouldn't fancy our chances with your Sammy.'

'So?' said Jimmy. 'What yer sayin'?'

'I'm sayin' there's bin a change of plan,' said Pete, pointing at Rose who was banging her fists against the wall.

'No,' said Jimmy, as Pete lurched towards Rose. 'Don't touch 'er. It'll be OK. Give 'er time. She'll . . .'

Pete had reached the wall and made a grab at Rose. She ducked underneath his outstretched arm and headed for the door. Both men lunged at her. Pete got there first.

'Oh, God,' said Jimmy. 'Now look what you've gone and done.'

Both men stared at Rose's motionless body, stretched across the doorway. Jimmy picked her up and put her on the bed.

'Did yer 'ave to hit 'er like that?' he said. 'She's a kid. She's just a kid.'

He put his head down to Rose's chest.

'She's out cold. She's hardly breathing. Oh, God, feel her fingers. They're frozen. What if she . . .'

'She won't be able to say nothin' then, will she? I reckon we ought to finish it . . . What's that?'

'What?'

'I heard someone. I'm out of here, Jim boy.'

'Wait,' yelled Jimmy, as Pete pulled the door open.

Pete stopped sharp at the top of the stairs. Jimmy, in his hurry to be gone crashed into him. Pete grabbed the rail to stop himself falling. Both men stared at the teenagers standing on the half-landing where the stairs curved round.

'What have you done?' Mandy screamed. 'What have you done to Rose?'

'We didn't mean to,' said Jimmy. 'It were an accident . . . she . . .'

'Shut it!' Pete yelled at him. 'We didn't do nothin'. Now back off before yer get hurt.'

Pete had pulled a knife from his pocket to emphasize his point.

'Geroff,' said Jimmy. 'They're only a couple of kids. Yer don't need that. They're movin'. Aren't yer?'

Mandy glanced at J'hon. He was trying to establish eye contact with the older man. Too late. Pete was quicker than the boys in the alley had been. He leapt down the stairs and lunged at J'hon, thrusting the knife at his stomach.

Mandy screamed.

J'hon didn't double over or try to protect himself. He stood up perfectly straight and still. The knife made contact and broke. Mandy's mouth stayed open as the scream died in her throat. Her mind sifted images, searching for rational explanations of the totally inexplicable. Muscle control. She'd seen body builders do similar tricks with muscle control, but J'hon was no Mr Universe.

Pete's less enquiring mind didn't even bother looking for answers. His slow-moving eyes glanced at the handle he was clutching as his ears caught the sound of the blade clattering down the stairs. He looked up, bemused, and was caught, for a moment, by the orange glow from J'hon's eyes. Recovering, he edged away, down the stairs, closely followed by Jimmy.

'Do something,' Mandy screamed. 'They're getting away.'

J'hon waited until they reached the landing below before steadily focusing his eyes on them again. Before Mandy could see what, if anything, had happened, he grabbed her hand and together they raced towards an open door.

Rose lay on the bed where Jimmy had left her. Colour drained from Mandy's face when she saw her. Both girls were as white as the stark walls which surrounded them.

J'hon sat on the edge of the bed. Mandy slumped to her knees on the bare floor, expecting to see the gloves come off and the nails twist into syringes and scalpels.

Nothing happened.

'Do something,' Mandy whispered, clutching Rose's hand. 'Make her better, J'hon. Like you did for Meg.'

J'hon smiled. His thoughts settled into Mandy's head as if they were her own.

'To help Meg was easy. For Rose, pain

more deep inside. Bruises heal OK,' he said brushing his hand against Rose's discoloured cheek. 'But for the rest, you must help.'

'How?' said Mandy, barely able to think as she watched the bruise fade at each sweep of J'hon's hand.

'Talk with her, while I work,' he said, pressing his hands onto Rose's forehead. 'Make her accept me.'

'What do I say . . . I . . .'

There was no answer. J'hon was already lost, his eyes fixed on Rose's face.

'Rose,' she began. 'It's Mandy. Don't be frightened. I've brought someone to help you. Let him help you, Rose. Don't fight him. Let him help you. It'll be all right. I promise. Everything's going to be all right.'

But would it? What was she doing? What was J'hon doing? How could she expose Rose to something she didn't understand? Something that could be dangerous.

'Don't do that!' J'hon's voice shouted. 'Don't doubt me. Help me. Talk to her. Keep talking.'

'Rose,' she began again. 'Rose. It's me. Mandy. I've come to help you . . . J'hon's a friend . . .'

Mandy wasn't sure how long she sat there, in the small, dark room, holding Rose, talking to her, reassuring her while J'hon . . . while J'hon did what? She didn't know what he was doing but gradually she felt Rose relax. All the tension slipped from her body. Colour came back into her pale cheeks. After what seemed like hours but was, maybe, only minutes, Rose opened her eyes and smiled.

'Mandy,' she said, peacefully and without surprise. 'Mandy. I've had such a lovely dream.'

J'hon lifted his hands and swept his fingertips across Rose's eyelids.

'She'll sleep now,' he told Mandy. 'And when she wakes, she'll be fine. More happy than she was before.'

'Will she remember?'

'Most things, yes. But she will accept the memories. They will not cause hurt.'

'How do you know? How can you be sure? How do you do the things you do?

How can you talk to me like this? Straight into my mind. Who are you?'

'So many questions,' he said, getting up and walking towards the boarded window, staring outwards as though he could see. 'And very little time, I think. Where would you like me to start?'

'With who you are.'

'This much you know. My name is J'hon. J'hon D'Harana.'

'And where . . .'

Mandy stopped.

'You see! You not really want to know. You know it will . . . how do you put it? Explode your mind.'

'I'll risk it,' said Mandy. 'Tell me.'

'I can't.'

'Can't or won't?'

'It would not be right for you to know. Already you know too much.'

'Too much! J'hon, I don't know anything.'

'OK. I tell you a story.'

'A story! I want information not a fairytale.'

'All right,' he said. 'No fairies. But imagine this. Imagine a world. A world very like yours is now. Divided, troubled, plagued by war and disease. A world inhabited by beings who, with all their problems, still thought themselves pretty smart, yes? They had made computers and sent their first satellites into deep space. Satellites discovered by more clever beings.'

'Who pick up our signals and come and visit us? Is that what you're saying?'

'Wait,' said J'hon. 'Remember I not talk of Earth. Only of an imaginary world which was very much like it. A world which the more clever beings looked down on and pitied.'

'OK,' said Mandy. 'Go on.'

'So, the clever beings pitied it and passed it by, leaving it to evolve, in its own good time. Time which almost ran out. The atmosphere was in decay. Resources almost gone.'

'Sounds familiar,' said Mandy, dryly.

'This world was not able to help itself,' said J'hon, ignoring the interruption. 'It was not so smart as it thought. So one day, someone decided to help them. A very advanced race of creatures appeared to show this world how to put right its many problems. They were totally peaceful, these creatures. They looked a bit strange but inside they were beautiful, like angels. They gave the sick world technology they'd never dreamt of.'

'A happy ending then? We're back to fairytales.'

'Not quite. This world, which was very much like yours, took the gifts. Learnt to use the advanced technology and then turned it against themselves and their peace-loving friends.'

'Why?' said Mandy, beginning to be drawn into the story. 'Why would they do that?'

'Because they were not ready. It was like giving to children guns with real bullets to play with. Within ten years the world was a wasteland. Cities in ruins. Climate doing strange things. Most of the people dead or dying.'

'So what about their oh-so-advanced friends? Why didn't they stop it?'

'You not understand. They could do nothing. They could not deal with violence and destruction. Evil, once started, can be much stronger than good. So they withdrew. They had no choice.'

'OK, but what are you saying, J'hon? Where does this get us? What does this tell me about you?'

'It tells you everything,' he said. 'If you will only hear what I say.'

'I'm listening. I'm trying to understand. But I can't. Is this just a story or is it real? Are you talking about Earth? Is this something that might happen if . . . Are you trying to tell me . . . J'hon, what are you looking at?'

J'hon's eyes were still fixed in the distance, beyond the boarded-up window.

'I am almost out of time. Everything is closing in. Help for Rose is on the way. But them I can delay, for a moment, while we finish our story.'

CHAPTER TWELVE

The young police officer swung the unmarked police car sharply to the left. In the back Mr Jones fell against his wife, who, in turn, squashed Sue against the door.

'What on earth are you doing now?' Detective Superintendent Callaghan snapped at his driver.

'You said turn left.'

'I didn't say a word. You're supposed to know where you're going.'

'I do. We should have gone straight on but you said turn . . .'

'I tell you, I didn't say anything. Just like I didn't say anything when you took it into your head to go round that roundabout three times or right at those lights. What's wrong with you?'

'Nothing I . . .'

'Stop the car.'

The young man carried on driving.

'I said stop the car,' Callaghan yelled into his ear.

'Yes, but did you really say it?'

'Of course I really said it! Stop the car, I'll drive. I don't know,' he grumbled, sliding into the vacated driver's seat. 'Young cops. Crack at the slightest pressure. Hearing things, indeed.'

'I suppose mad women seeing pictures of blocks of flats is OK,' the young man muttered, as he slammed the door and walked round to the passenger side.

Callaghan checked his mirror and performed a quick three-point turn, bashing the rear wheels against the kerb.

'Want me to call for reinforcements?' the young officer said. 'And how about an ambulance? We don't know . . .'

'That's right,' Callaghan snapped. 'We don't know anything yet. I can't drag half the West Yorks force out on a wild goose chase because a couple of stressed-up women have been playing amateur psychics.'

'Now wait a minute,' said Sue, suddenly catching the drift of the conversation.

'Calm down,' said Callaghan. 'We're following this, because it's the only lead we've got, right? But I'm not going to stake my reputation on it. Let's just see what happens.'

'Er . . . sir . . .' said the young officer.

'What now?'

'Shouldn't you have gone straight on at those lights?'

'I did.'

'No, sir. You turned left.'

'I meant to go straight,' said Callaghan, a glance out of the window confirming that his colleague was right. 'What the heck's got into us all?'

J'hon left his post by the window and joined Mandy, sitting beside the sleeping Rose.

'That's it. That's all I can do. They'll have an accident if I mess around in their minds much more.'

'Whose minds?' said Mandy.

'Your police people and your parents. Your mother has strong telepathic sense, you know. She begins to pick up messages I not mean to send.'

'Mum!' said Mandy. 'Telepathic!'

'And Sue.'

'Sue?' Mandy repeated.

'Of course. To be telepathic is not so different to being empathic. You, your mother, Sue. You all have great experience of empathy with children who are distressed, like Rose. To develop this sense needs only a little push. It comes more easily to females of most species.'

'You're not female.'

'You very observant,' said J'hon. 'I'm happy you notice.'

'So how come you're so smart at it?'

'This imaginary world, I tell you about,' said J'hon, seemingly ignoring her question. 'I want to make fast my story. So I put a little picture in your mind. Yes?'

'I don't know . . . I . . . er . . .'

Before Mandy could finish, J'hon's fingers had swept across her temples. In that instant, Mandy felt as though someone had taken a pair of giant nut crackers and applied them to her head. A massive firework display exploded in front of her eyes. Then it was over.

In her mind was a new set of information. She knew the history of that so-called imaginary world as clearly as she knew her own. Seeing their development stretching back for generations. Back to the few, scattered survivors of their holocaust. Bereft, confused, denied the comforts of the technology which had destroyed them. No communications. No medicines. Contaminated food and water. The weakest died. The strongest began to adapt. Their bodies developed natural immunity. Self-healing properties which evolved into the ability to heal others, the way J'hon had healed Meg and Rose. The most successful survivors were those who learnt to communicate with other groups across vast distances of polluted wasteland, communicating first in feelings only, later in thoughts.

'Is this your history, J'hon?' she said, as the images began to settle. 'Is it your world you're telling me about? Or is it all made up? Is this your idea of what might happen to Earth in the future?'

'It is a story, I tell. It may have happened

somewhere. It may happen again. But imagine, Mandy, if there was a world like that? A world which had suffered because of well-meaning interference. A world which had come out from its near destruction, a little stronger and wiser, what would it do?'

'What do you mean?'

'If it knew there were other worlds now. Worlds like it was itself many millions of years ago. Worlds that could do with a little help . . .'

'It would leave them,' said Mandy. 'It would leave them alone. It wouldn't interfere.'

'Quite,' said J'hon. 'To interfere would not be allowed. And this would be quite right. But there would always be curious individuals who wanted to explore. Who were willing to break the rules. Just to have a closer look.'

Mandy nodded. Before she could speak, she felt the pressure of Rose's hand, gently squeezing her own.

'Rose?'

'Hello, Mandy,' she said, with the dreaminess of someone coming round from an operation. 'It's nice here. I feel so warm and happy.'

The eyes closed again. Mandy looked down at her face. It was so peaceful. After everything that had happened, she looked peaceful. Whoever J'hon was, whatever he had done – it was wonderful.

'So you see,' said J'hon. 'I not mean to do harm but already I am a danger.'

'How can you say that? You haven't done anything bad. Look at her, J'hon. Look at Rose. I've never seen her like that. When she was with us, I think she was happy, most of the time. But she was always tense and wary. Her shoulders were more or less permanently hunched, her forehead creased with anxiety and she never made direct eye contact, like she did a minute ago. It's brilliant! If you could help people to . . .'

'No,' he said. 'I'm happy to be able to help Rose. But no more. I must do nothing else. And all this must be kept secret. Soon someone will come for me. I sense their presence very strong. One day, one night, I will seem simply to disappear. You must not worry. You must tell your parents that I run away, as I think many young people do. You must never tell what you think you know. You have to forget everything that has happened.'

'Oh, sure,' said Mandy. 'That'll be real easy. A crazy boy walks into my life. I see his nails perform some advanced animal surgery, he reads my mind, tells me incredible stories about . . .'

'Sssh. I hear them. Your parents. Your police.'

'I don't hear . . . Wait a minute, yes I do. J'hon, what are we going to say, how are we going to explain?'

'Relax,' J'hon said, holding her hands and touching her lips with his own. 'You will know what to say.'

Mandy's body relaxed instantly, her mind clear and calm. It stayed calm as she heard the footsteps bounding up the stairs. She managed a reassuring smile when her parents and Sue rushed into the room.

'They're here. We've found them,' Sue shouted, darting out again.

Mandy's father wrapped his arms round her. Her mother sank onto the bed, almost crushing Rose in her embrace.

'Is she . . .'

'She's fine, Mum,' said Mandy. 'At least she was until you jumped on her. Look.'

Rose had opened her eyes and was attempting to sit up.

'Oh, thank God,' said Mandy's father. 'I thought we'd lost you both. When we bumped into those weirdos down in the hall, I was sure . . .'

'I'd forgotten about them,' said Mandy. 'With everything else . . .'

'Are they the ones?' said her father. 'I couldn't make out whether they were involved in this or just a couple of addicts who'd taken shelter. They were behaving very strangely . . . crawling round the floor . . . chasing imaginary tails or something.'

'I wonder why that was?' said Mandy, looking at J'hon again. 'You'd think they'd have tried to get away. Probably drugs, like Dad says.'

'Is J'hon all right?' said Mr Jones, noticing

him for the first time. 'And how the heck did you two know Rose was here?'

'J'hon's fine and . . . er . . .'

It came to Mandy with perfect clarity. As though someone had slotted the lie neatly into her mind.

'We got an anonymous phone call,' she said. 'At the house. After Mum had left. About five minutes after J'hon turned up. Said we'd find Rose here but not to bring the cops or she'd get hurt.'

'Yeah, that's right. I made that phone call. That's what I said.'

Mandy turned to the door to see the source of this unexpected confirmation of her lie. The two kidnappers stood, leaning unsteadily against the two police officers, with Sue hovering behind.

'Kid weren't well,' Jimmy went on. 'I was worried. She kept shoutin' out for – er – Mandy, aren't it? So I phoned.'

Pete looked at him as menacingly as he could manage out of glazed, bloodshot eyes.

'When? . . . How? . . . Might 'ave known yer'd mess up on me, yer cretin,' he snarled at Jimmy.

His anger made him weak. He staggered forward. J'hon stretched out his arm.

'Keep 'im off me,' Pete yelled, as Callaghan pulled him upright again. 'Get him out of my head. He's in there. I can feel him . . .'

'Odd,' said Callaghan, as Mandy's stomach dropped to her toes. 'Never known these two do drugs before. More your sort of twelve pints and a bit of GBH types. But they're sure on something now. Never seen anything quite like it. You should have heard what they were saying down there. Saw a spaceship, apparently. Right out there, on the estate, didn't you, Jim?'

'Spaceship?' said Mandy.

She looked at J'hon and saw, for an instant, an emotion she'd seen from him once before, when the phone rang. It was terror.

'Oh yes,' said the police officer. 'They definitely saw a spaceship. Apparently we're about to be invaded by aliens.'

Callaghan nodded towards J'hon.

'Your friend here's one of them,' he said, laughing.

Mandy managed a forced giggle to join in

the general merriment which had erupted as a result of this statement.

'What are aliens?' Rose suddenly asked.

Mrs Jones lifted her from the bed and held her close.

'Nothing, sweetheart. Nothing for you to worry about. We ought to get her . . . Sue, what's going to happen now?'

Cath passed Rose to Mandy, as Sue drew her to one side.

'We've got enough evidence of neglect to take her into care again. Mike's been round at Babs's. I think she's decided it won't work. It's a shame in a way. At one time, I really thought Babs was going to make a go of it. But it was all too much for her. She knows that now. I don't think she'll contest if you still want to . . .'

'Oh yes,' said Cath. 'We do.'

Rose clutched Mandy as the sound of sirens wailed across the estate growing ever louder, nearer.

'Thought we asked them to keep a low profile,' said Callaghan.

'How did you find us so quickly?' Mandy asked.

'It was funny,' said her mother.

J'hon looked at her and smiled.

'Funny,' she continued. 'Because . . . er . . . What was it, Sue?'

Sue shook her head, in confusion.

'Not much we can't do, these days,' said Callaghan confidently. 'All down to technology, young lady. Scientific investigation.'

'What about the ambulance?' said the younger officer, as a different siren was heard. 'Shall I send it back? The girl seems fine.'

'We might need it for these two,' said Callaghan, still supporting Jimmy. 'They seem to be coming round a bit now, though. Come on. Let's get them downstairs.'

'Can you walk?' Mandy asked, lowering Rose to the floor. 'If I hold your hand?'

'Course,' said Rose, smiling first at Mandy and then, less certainly, at J'hon.

'This is J'hon,' said Mandy. 'He's staying with us . . . for a while.'

'I know,' said Rose. 'He's an a—'

'Ssssh,' said Mandy, kneeling beside Rose, as the grown-ups trooped out after

Callaghan. 'Whatever you know about J'hon is our secret . . . yes?'

Rose nodded.

'But I know what they are,' she whispered.

'What?' said Mandy.

'Aliens,' she said, proudly. 'I know what they are. They make dreams. Lovely dreams.'

'Yes,' said Mandy, looking at J'hon. 'I suppose they do.'

CHAPTER THIRTEEN

Mandy stood with J'hon and her parents in the garden, watching Rose play.

'I can't believe she's so well,' said Mrs Jones. 'After everything she's been through. But the doctor said she was in great shape. Says she can go back to school tomorrow.'

Rose had spent Thursday quietly at home. On Friday she had seen a doctor and been interviewed by the police. Mandy and J'hon had been packed off to school as usual. On Saturday they had brought Gran home from hospital. The hip replacement had been a success. In a few months she would be back to normal. Not bad. But not good enough for J'hon. He was itching to intervene. Confident that he could accelerate the healing process to just a few days.

Mandy watched Meg race across the lawn after a ball. It was tempting. That was the trouble. There were too many temptations. Too many things J'hon had to stop himself doing. Already people were getting suspicious.

Rose, too young to know the meaning of discretion, kept talking about her experiences.

'J'hon showed me what happened,' she confided to Mandy's father. 'What happened when my first mum died and everything. But I don't feel sad. Not any more. I understand now. J'hon told me . . .'

'Told you? Did he write something down?'

'No. He told me.'

'But J'hon can't talk, love,' Mr Jones had said.

'Yes he can. But you listen with your head, not your ears. It's easy.'

Mr Jones had smiled, allowing Rose her fantasies, as he assumed them to be. But it was all rather unnerving. So far, with the worry about Rose, nobody had bothered too much about J'hon. But they would, if he stayed around.

J'hon turned to look at Mandy. He could

sense her thoughts all the time. It was sort of weird, this lack of privacy. She'd started censoring her thoughts, as she would her speech, only allowing herself complete freedom when she was well away from J'hon.

'So what's happening?' she asked him. 'What are you going to do?'

He shrugged and turned away.

'Don't do that!' she hissed at him. 'Don't shut me out. Not now. Let's go somewhere. Somewhere on our own. Where we can talk.'

They went to the hills above the park.

'So?' said Mandy.

'So?' J'hon's voice came back.

'What now? It's getting tricky. You must see that. Either you've got to open up, give us some real explanations or . . .'

'I already tell you. No problem. I go soon.'

'OK – but how soon? You said someone would come for you but how, when, who? Your parents?'

'Parents? No. I have no parents.'

'I'm sorry . . .'

'No,' said J'hon. 'Not to be sorry. You

misunderstand. For me it is natural. I have lived alone since very young.'

'But that's terrible!'

'Different. Not terrible. Like some of your baby animals. They do not cling to parents and families. Frogs for an example, they lay their spawn . . .'

'J'hon, I know what frogs do. I don't need a biology lesson. But you're not a frog.'

'Correct.'

'Don't distract me. I'm thinking! So you have no parents. But you must have a home. Don't you want to go home?'

'No.'

'Why not? Is it so bad? Will you be in trouble? Will . . .'

'Not so fast. First, it is not, as you put it, so bad. You might, in some ways, call it a paradise. But a lonely one. We long ago stopped living in groups. We spend much time on our own. Most like it that way. "Contact leads to Conflict" is our first Rule of Remembrance. But, for some of us, it is restricting. We like to know. To explore. We take risks which are against the Rules of Remembrance.'

'And if you're caught?'

'Caught?' said J'hon, laughing. 'No-one catches anyone else. They will come and I will go with them as I know I must. But, for a while, I put them off the smell.'

'Scent.'

'Yes, I put them off,' he said. 'But don't look so worried. We are not barbarians, like you. Nothing bad will happen to me. I will go back only when I absolutely must. For, after that, it will be made very difficult for me to travel again.'

'Do you know what I think?' said Mandy, looking at him quizzically.

'Yes. And it is not very flattering to me!'

'Sorry. I forget sometimes. But it could be true, couldn't it? You could just be some loony who's escaped from an institution. Like these guys who think they're Napoleon or Elvis . . . or little green men from Alpha Centauri. You could be making all this up.'

'Fine. I make it all up. Think as you like.'

'I'm sorry. But you're so . . . so . . . I don't know what to think.'

'Perhaps think nothing. Just accept me.

Don't push me to go. I want to stay, Mandy. I'd like always to stay.'

The words were familiar. The pleading tone the same. It had been in Sarah's voice two years ago when she'd been told she was too old for foster care. She had heard it from Ben, when he returned to his mother and the stepfather he hated. Some were pleased to go home. Others weren't. It didn't matter. The decisions were always made by someone else. As J'hon's would be.

'But you can't, can you? You said . . .'

Suddenly J'hon was staring at her. Tears in his eyes.

'Don't hide behind words, Mandy. You can't. Not with me. You don't want me, do you? I'm too weird. You don't want me to stay.'

The accusation floated on the air.

'You don't want me to stay.'

It was not J'hon's voice she heard but Lucy's, after the episode with the car. After she'd shredded every item in Mandy's wardrobe and smeared excreta over the bedroom walls. After she'd been expelled from three local schools. When the social

166

workers decided to return her to the children's home. She had blamed Mandy.

Mandy leaned forward as she felt the pain. The pain that always came when she had to say goodbye. Even the kids she had thought she'd hated. Even Lucy. She hadn't wanted her around. She couldn't cope with Lucy. No-one could. But it had hurt when she left.

She felt J'hon's arms around her shoulders. 'I'm sorry . . . I make you think of . . .'

'No,' she said, pushing him away. 'It's not your fault. It happens sometimes. There are kids who . . . well, it just doesn't work out.'

'What happened – with Lucy – after she left you?'

Mandy shook her head, fighting back the knowledge which threatened to rise to the surface. It was enough for J'hon. He had already seen.

'I'm sorry,' he said again. 'You have many problems. I won't cause more. I'll take care . . . not to be so noticed.'

'You are joking!' said Mandy. 'You've already been noticed. You skate like a professional, play chess like a Grand Master.'

'That was before I knew what is normal. I will be less good at things, yes?'

'It's not as easy as that. You can't hold back. Pretend all the time.'

'But I'll try . . .'

'They all try,' said Mandy bitterly. 'Lucy tried. But sometimes it's just not good enough. You can't change what you are, J'hon, any more than Lucy could. You're just not like other people.'

'I know. And you know. The more you can accept me, the more I will be able to tell you. But it will be our secret. I will be careful not to let anything bad happen, I promise.'

'Where have I heard that before?' Mandy muttered, turning to walk back across the hills towards home. 'And why am I stupid enough to believe it?'

They walked in silence, Mandy trying to quieten the chaos of thoughts she knew J'hon could hear. There were people, all over the world, who claimed to have seen spaceships, to have met aliens – been abducted by them, even. She had always dismissed them as lunatics. And now, here she was, slithering down a grassy slope, clutching the hand of . . .

'Interesting,' she heard him say. 'Part of your defence mechanism. You refuse to accept what you cannot understand.'

'Don't talk about me as though I'm a specimen!'

'Sorry,' he said but there was laughter in his voice, where apology should have been.

At the bottom of the hill the long road towards home stretched out in front of them. It was quiet. It was always quiet on a Sunday afternoon. Just one old lady walking her terrier and someone further down, waving.

Waving. Mandy looked again at the familiar figure rushing towards them.

'Dad!' she shouted.

Her face turned pale, as she dragged J'hon to meet him. Her dad never hurried. There must be something wrong. Gran? Rose?

'It's all right,' her father assured her, as they met. 'Nothing's wrong. In fact it's good news, I think. Mike's just turned up with J'hon's parents.'

'Parents?' Mandy squeaked.

She looked at J'hon, who raised his eyebrows but remained silent. He rarely used his telepathy with another person so close, even someone as unreceptive as Mandy's dad.

'You've seen them?' Mandy asked, turning her attention to her dad.

'Yes, they're at the house.'

'Are you sure?'

'Mandy, I know whether I've seen someone or not!'

'No, I mean are you sure they're his parents? Can they prove it?'

'Well, Mike's satisfied. They turned up two days ago with all the right documents. Birth certificate. Photographs. Passports.'

'Two days ago? Dad, did you know about this?'

'I heard yesterday but I was told not to say anything until . . .'

'Well you should have told me,' Mandy snapped. 'Then I could have told you something. They're not his parents. J'hon doesn't have any parents.'

'Mandy,' her dad whispered. 'You know

what these kids are like. They don't always tell the truth. Remember little Stevie? He told all sorts of stories about his parents being killed in plane crashes and skiing accidents. Anything so he didn't have to face up to their divorce.'

'J'hon's not like that,' Mandy hissed. 'He doesn't have any parents. I know he doesn't.'

'He does, love. It all checks out. And their story fits your theory about Jan.'

'Jan?'

'Yes, that's his name. Jan, not J'hon. The family are of East European descent. And Jan's – er – well, he's got special needs . . . some condition. Can't remember the name. Similar to autism, like you said. He's extremely bright. Gifted. But he's rather unstable,' said her father, so quietly she could barely hear. 'Exhibits severe behavioural disturbance sometimes. Compulsive liar. Makes up amazing stories about himself.'

'So this severely unstable son's been gone more than two weeks and they've only just reported him missing?' Mandy asked.

'Keep your voice down. He understands everything. All that business with language was a game. He understands English perfectly. Always has. He can even talk when he's a mind to, they say. He's got a special way of speaking which suits his short tongue.'

'Fine,' Mandy shouted. 'He speaks. He understands. And he deserves to hear this pack of lies. Now how about answering my question. How come they've only just noticed he's missing?'

'There was some mix up apparently,' said Mandy's dad calmly. 'His parents are travellers. Entertainers.'

'Really?' said Mandy, cynically. 'With a circus by any chance?'

'Yes, as it happens. Family have been in the circus for generations. Jan too, until recently. He's got some amazing talents, physically and mentally. But he's prone to blackouts. Fits. Bouts of amnesia. Makes it dangerous. So for the past year he's been staying with a retired couple on the East Coast.'

'Mike's checked, of course?'

'Of course. Anyway, Jan was spending some time with his parents when the circus was in Bradford. A friend was supposed to take him back to his carers. Somehow Jan persuaded the friend to tell the carers he was staying on with his parents. And off he went on a little adventure. It was lucky he landed up with us. Anything could have happened to him. Last time . . .'

'Last time?'

'Oh, yes. He's done it several times before. About six months ago they found him in a squat with some drug addicts. He was in a real mess. Made him more unstable than ever. Almost died.'

'Did he?' said Mandy, her voice brimming with disbelief. 'And doesn't anything strike you as odd about all this?'

'Like what?'

'Like every flaming bit of it. But try this for starters. Their story doesn't just fit one of my theories, does it? It fits all of them. Everything I've ever said about J'hon is in there, as if they picked it straight out of my mind.'

'Out of your mind?' said her dad, putting

his arm round her shoulder. 'Mandy, love, please. I know you're upset. You've had a lot of stress lately. But think what you're saying? A couple of people, who don't even know you, pick thoughts out of your mind? Their story fits your theories because you're good at working things out. You understand these kids. Sue always says you'd make a great social worker. It's crazy to think . . .'

'Crazy,' said Mandy, tearing herself away. 'You're probably right. I'm probably going mad but I'll tell you one thing. They're not his parents. I know they're not.'

CHAPTER FOURTEEN

They were waiting in the kitchen. He wore a dark coat and leather driving gloves. She was clutching his arm, her beige gloves resting on his sleeve. They were both dark haired, dusky skinned. A good genetic match for J'hon. Apart from the eyes. Their eyes were normal. Deep brown. No excess colour.

'Jan!' the lady cried. 'Jan!'

Both parents began to talk at once but Mandy barely heard the words. She was too busy watching their mouths. They both spoke tight-lipped, like puppets. Was it her imagination or were the words slightly out of time with the movement, like some dubbed foreign film? Was this real speech or mime to projected thoughts?

Speech, she told herself. Perfectly ordinary speech. Perfectly ordinary people.

'Are these your parents, Jan?' Mike Patty was asking.

J'hon nodded in weary resignation. Then he made an effort to look pleased.

'It's time to go home, Jan,' the lady said. 'It's all arranged.'

'Wait a minute,' said Mandy. 'There's a few things I'd like to know.'

J'hon shook his head.

'Mandy, please,' said her mother.

'It's all right,' said the lady in the beige gloves. 'We've had this before. Jan can be very convincing. What is it you'd like to know, dear?'

'Nothing,' said Mandy. 'Forget it.'

'Has he been trying the telepathy trick on you?' she asked, sympathetically.

'Trick?' Mandy repeated, looking at J'hon.

'You know how ventriloquists throw their voice?' the woman said.

'No,' said Mandy. 'I mean yes but . . .'

'Jan can do that. He does it so well, you hear his voice without seeing his lips move at all. It's a way of speaking he developed because of his tongue.'

Mandy looked at her in confusion. She wanted to argue but didn't quite know what to say.

'So what about his tongue,' she managed to mumble. 'And his eyes. How come he looks that way?'

The woman's head drooped. It was the man who spoke.

'My wife . . . it upsets her. She feels guilty about the way J'hon is. She was working while pregnant . . . had a fall . . . With the shock and the drugs they gave her – well, we think that accounts for the physical problems. As for the rest . . .'

'Like mind reading?' Mandy snapped. 'I don't suppose that's a ventriloquist trick or birth defect, is it?'

'Observation and clever guesswork,' the lady said, wearily. 'Any stage mindreader could tell you that. And Jan's been taught by the best. I'm sorry, if you've been taken in, dear. Jan's so very talented. He'd make a fine performer if he wasn't so unpredictable. I'm just glad he didn't have one of his fits while he was with you and thank you,' she said, turning her attention to Mandy's parents. 'Thank you for taking such good care of him.'

'Is J'hon going?' Rose asked, anxiously, wrapping her arms round Mandy's waist.

'It looks that way,' Mandy whispered, trying to stay calm for Rose's sake. 'Sometimes people have to go home. Sometimes it's best.'

'But not me,' said Rose. 'I don't have to go, do I? We're sisters now, aren't we? Real sisters?'

'Yes,' said Mandy. 'We're real sisters and you don't have to go anywhere.'

It wasn't true. Not quite. They had begun the adoption procedure once again but these things took time. It could be a year, two years or more before it was finalized. But it would be. This time, Babs wouldn't contest. There had been a time when this would have filled Mandy with sheer delight. Now she wasn't so sure. Babs couldn't cope. She had neglected Rose, as her parents had once done. But she did love her in her own way.

Mandy shook her head. Was this J'hon's influence or was she simply growing up?

One thing was certain. It was easier to hate Babs than to try to understand.

'Much easier.'

J'hon's voice came quietly into her head, like an echo of her own. So quiet that she almost missed it. He kissed Rose's forehead, whilst gently unravelling her arms from Mandy's waist.

'I'm just going outside,' Mandy told Rose. 'I want to talk to J'hon. OK?'

They leant on the garden gate, their heads close together.

'Why, J'hon?' Mandy said. 'Why did you lie to me? You didn't have to. I liked you. I'd have accepted you just as you are. The things you can do – your gifts – they're wonderful. You didn't have to tell me all those crazy stories.'

J'hon looked at her but said nothing.

'I'm not angry,' said Mandy. 'Maybe I should be, but I'm not. And I meant what I said. I like you. You're the cleverest, craziest person I've ever met. And I want to see you again. So keep in touch, OK?'

J'hon's bright eyes filled with tears.

'I can't.'

'Yes, you can. There's nothing to stop you. I'll get your address from Mike and Sue. I'll write.'

'I won't reply,' his voice said, sadly. 'And you'll think it's because I don't want to. But it won't be that. Don't you realize, Mandy? No letter on Earth will reach me.'

'Stop it. Stop that. It's not fair. I believed you, you know. I really believed all that rubbish.'

'I never told you any lies.'

'Not lies maybe. But you let me believe . . .'

'And now you believe what they say? My so-called parents. I suppose it is to be expected. They have powers,' said J'hon, 'stronger than mine. They . . .'

He stopped. People were drifting out. Standing by the back door.

'J'hon, do you have to go?' Mandy said urgently. 'You could deny they're your parents. You . . .'

'There would be enquiries,' J'hon said. 'Investigations. I could not risk that. It would expose all of us to dreadful possibilities.'

'Expose you, you mean,' said Mandy. 'Give me a chance to find out what a fraud you are!' She laughed. 'You're brilliant, you know that. You really had me taken in. My friend the Martian! You must think I'm a real idiot.'

'No.'

'Take care, J'hon,' she said, suddenly grabbing his hand. 'I don't care who you are or what you've done. I'll miss you.'

Miss you. Words she had said so many times before. It didn't make them less real. She would miss J'hon as she missed all the others. Sarah, Ben, little Billy, even Lucy.

'J'hon,' she whispered, as Rose raced towards them. 'Stop the game now. Stop the pretence. Tell me . . .'

But it was too late. Rose was there. Everyone was there. In an instant, it was over. The gates opened. The car doors opened.

Mandy watched through blurred eyes as the car pulled away. She didn't know what she'd expected, what she believed. Had she hoped to see J'hon disappear in a flying saucer or a blaze of light? To see what Jimmy Hutchins claimed to have seen on the night of the kidnap? The grand finale which ended all sci-fi films? She didn't know. But one thing was for sure. It was strange to see him driven away in an old, blue Ford.

They came at night. The doorbell and Meg's barking drew Mandy back from the brink of sleep. She looked over to the bed in the corner. Rose slept on.

It was six weeks since J'hon had left. The pain was fading. Yet the questions remained. Her parents and the social workers firmly believed that J'hon was nothing more than a highly disturbed, yet gifted, adolescent. Mandy had believed it at first too. But, as time passed, what J'hon's parents had claimed made less and less sense. What her own parents believed barely accounted for one half of J'hon's abilities. But then, they hadn't seen what Mandy had seen and she hadn't tried to tell them.

How could she? Those nails for instance. Real or imagined? His work with Rose and Meg? Effective or lucky coincidence? Her telepathic link with J'hon. Not just some corny stage act, surely? Yet if she'd confided in her parents? Tried to say what she thought was the truth? They'd have booked an appointment with a psychologist before she'd reached the end of the first sentence. So, in the end, she'd settled for secrecy and a few general enquiries.

'Have you checked on Jan since his parents took him?' she'd asked Mike. 'I'd like an address. I want to write.'

'Ah. Tricky. I tried to.'

'Tried to?'

'Tried to check. They were supposed to join the circus down in Devon but they never turned up.'

'And the carers on the East Coast?'

'Mmmm,' Mike had said, stroking his beard. 'That was a bit odd.'

'Go on. Amaze me.'

'They've gone. Moved, I suppose. Didn't tell anyone.'

'So there's actually no trace of Jan or his family or his carers?'

'Not as yet but there's no reason to suspect foul play. They'll turn up, somewhere,

I'm sure. And we'll keep the file open, of course.'

'You'll tell me if you find them, Mike? I need to know, OK?'

Mike had promised to let her know. But if he didn't trace them? What then? What was she left with? A mystery. An enigma.

She shook her head, shaking away the uncomfortable thoughts which made her question her own sanity. It didn't matter, she told herself, firmly. What she'd shared with J'hon was unique. Wonderful. She felt fine. They had got Rose back. Life had settled to pleasant normality.

Mandy's head flopped back onto the pillow, her eyes closed. She drifted back into peaceful . . .

Not peaceful. Something was wrong. The voices. Mike and Sue. Mandy glanced at the luminous numbers on the alarm clock. Eleven fifteen. Social workers visiting at eleven fifteen could only mean one thing. Trouble.

Wrapped in an unsettling mist of *déjà-vu*, Mandy clambered out of bed, put on her slippers and wandered to the top of the stairs.

After J'hon they had promised. No more special cases. No more children. Not until Rose had had time to settle again. Until Mandy had done her exams. Exams which were still over a year away.

Sue's voice became clear as Mandy reached the middle of the stairs.

'I should have phoned first . . . We wouldn't normally . . . I mean I know what you said . . . but you're the only ones who could possibly . . . Going to a new foster home would be too traumatic. The only hope is to try again here.'

'Here. Try again. Here.'

The words echoed in Mandy's head, impeding her progress as she stumbled down the final steps, tripped over the dog and crashed through the lounge door. It could only mean one thing. He was back. J'hon was back.

The scene was the same. Adults sitting. Young figure standing, frozen in the middle of the room. Back turned to Mandy. Dark hair, roughly tied up. Dark clothes.

Only this time Mandy's crashed entrance could not be ignored. The figure turned. Thinner than Mandy remembered. Much thinner. A little older. Livid scars on the right wrist, visible as the hand began to tug, nervously, at a loose strand of hair around the ear.

Mandy recovered her balance and just enough of her composure to speak as she moved towards the girl.

'Hi, Lucy,' she said.

'It don't matter,' said Lucy, shrugging her shoulders. 'I knew you wouldn't 'ave me back. I told 'em. It was 'er that said we'd try,' she added, nodding towards Sue.

'I should have given you more warning,' Sue said, though without a trace of apology. 'Police picked her up. She's been . . . well it could be a criminal charge. So it's either this or a secure unit.'

'I don't mind,' Lucy said. 'It don't matter. They don't want me. Let's go.'

Mandy struggled with her disappoint-ment. It wasn't J'hon. Crazy to think he would come back. She looked at her parents looking at her. Mum was weakening already, Lucy was scared. So vulnerable despite all the tough talk.

They knew the history. Sue and Mike had kept them informed. Since leaving them eighteen months ago, Lucy had become anorexic. She had twice attempted suicide. A month ago she had absconded from the children's home. Heaven knows what she had been doing since then. Whatever it was, Lucy was trouble. It hadn't worked out before and it wouldn't work out now.

'Don't say it,' Lucy snapped at her. 'I know what yer thinking. Just don't say it. You don't have to say it.'

Mandy's mind returned, involuntarily, to J'hon. Maybe he wasn't so very different. This ability to empathize, to read thoughts and feelings, was inherent in everyone. Not so strong as in J'hon but it was there. You didn't have to be an alien to sense Lucy's loneliness, to know her pain.

'We've had the spare room decorated,' Mandy said, to no-one in particular.

'I'd only muck it up,' said Lucy. 'If I stayed.'

'You'd have to go to school,' said Mandy's mother.

'If they'd have me.'

'We could try,' said Mandy, picking up the carrier bag which contained Lucy's belongings.

'And Rose is back. Remember Rose?' Mandy asked as she led Lucy upstairs. 'She was here before. Then, after you left, she went to . . .'

Lucy half listened to Mandy's story, whilst tipping her things onto the bed, opening cupboards, touching the new wallpaper and lighting a cigarette.

Mandy found a small pot to serve as an ashtray. Mum didn't allow smoking but that was her province. Mum would do battle with Lucy over the rules.

'There's only been one other person in here, since we decorated,' said Mandy, picking up the discarded, empty cigarette packet and throwing it into the bin. 'A boy. About our age. Called J'hon.'

Lucy lay on the bed, puffing at her cigarette, making no comment.

'I'll tell you about him sometime,' said Mandy.

'Liked 'im, did you?' said Lucy.

'Yes,' said Mandy. 'Yes I did.'

'Where'd he go, then?'

For a moment Mandy wondered what to say. In the end, she decided on the simple option. The story she had told at school.

'He went home.'

'See him again, will ya?'

'No. I don't think so.'

'Like that, is it?' said Lucy stubbing out her cigarette. 'Boys. Typical. Take my advice. Forget him.'

''Night, Lucy,' said Mandy, smiling.

Forget him. No, she wouldn't forget. She knew that for sure. She remembered every kid they'd ever fostered. Every kind of trauma they'd suffered. Every kind of disturbance. And not one, not even Lucy, came close to being as weird as J'hon.

Mandy pushed open the bedroom door, gently, so as not to disturb Rose. Would J'hon ever come back? Impossible to tell.

She peeped out of the bedroom curtain. It was dark. Totally black. No moon. No stars. Hard to believe there was anything or anybody out there. Even when you knew.

THE END

PIG-HEART BOY
Malorie Blackman

*All I had to do was go downstairs. Or I could
call Dad and tell him that I didn't want to meet
Dr Bryce and that would be the end of that. Life
would go on as normal. And I'd be dead before
my fourteenth birthday . . .*

Cameron is thirteen and desperately in
need of a heart transplant when a
pioneering doctor approaches his family
with a startling proposal. He can give
Cameron a new heart – but not from a
human donor. From a *pig*.

It's never been done before. It's
experimental, risky and *very* controversial.
But Cameron is fed up with just sitting on
the side of life, always watching and never
doing. He *has* to try – to become the world's
first pig-heart boy . . .

'A powerful story about friendship, loyalty
and family around this topical and
controversial issue' *Guardian*

'Blackman is becoming a bit of a national
treasure' *The Times*

0 552 52841 2

CORGI BOOKS